"You are determined to waste your time then?"

Lord Nathan Hatherleigh studied Kitty's face intently as it turned every shade of red.

"I don't think I shall be wasting my time," she said, fuming. "Why...why I'll just wager Sir William will not find me so unsuitable a wife as..."

"Just what will you wager, Miss Whitchurch?" Lord Hatherleigh interjected softly.

Lord Hatherleigh's complete lack of belief in her abilities was so utterly exasperating. However, Kitty knew she had nothing in the world of value to wager and was on the verge of telling the wretched beast so when he continued.

"I'll take Jezebel. She's a fine piece of horseflesh, that one."

Kitty was in a rage. She did not want to lose her horse, but she would vastly enjoy showing the earl that she was not just a silly, hoydenish girl from the country, unable to attract a city beau! She turned to face him with a militant glare in her clear green eyes.

"Done," she said emphatically. "And what will you wager, my lord?"

Lord Hatherleigh's smile was supremely smug as he answered with total confidence. "Why, myself, of course."

A COUNTRY CHIT

EMILY DALTON

Harlequin Books

TORONTO • NEW YORK • LONDON
AMSTERDAM • PARIS • SYDNEY • HAMBURG
STOCKHOLM • ATHENS • TOKYO • MILAN

Dedicated with love
to my husband, Allen,
and my two wonderful boys,
Christopher and Aaron

Published August 1990

ISBN 0-373-31131-1

CHAPTER ONE

"GOOD GAD, KITTY! Put down that gun!" demanded Benjamin Whitchurch, his soft white hands splayed cautiously in front of his chest.

"I should be happy to accommodate you, cousin. But first kindly explain why you stand devoid of breeches in my bedchamber at this ungodly hour!"

Moonlight streamed across the pale expanse of Kitty's counterpane and clearly illuminated her slender form propped up against the mahogany headboard. A sheet was tucked beneath her arms and drawn tightly across her front. Lying against her thigh, in stark contrast to its background, was her large black cat, Cleopatra, and clutched between her hands was a small, pearl-handled pistol.

"You know why I'm here." Benjamin licked his lips and wiped his palms on his nightshirt. "And I feel certain you will enjoy it excessively. I'm aware your reluctance this far has been due to regard for Sarah's feelings. But she's asleep, Kitty! There is absolutely no way she could hear us from so far down the hall, though your cries of ecstasy may indeed fill the room!"

Kitty's face contorted with repugnance. "Be quiet, Benjamin," she muttered unevenly, striving for at least some semblance of composure. "You are making me ill." She swallowed convulsively. "It sickens me to breathe the same air as you, and each drop of venom spilling from your lips is poison to my stomach."

"Lips that long to touch yours, Kitty. All of you..." He stepped forward tentatively.

Kitty lifted the gun slightly and leveled it at his heart. She marvelled that she held the weapon so steadily. Inwardly she trembled at what she might have to do.

"You are right about one thing, cousin," she conceded. "I have wished to spare Sarah's feelings, and for that reason I have avoided telling her the truth about you. But if you think I would allow you to turn your lascivious imaginings into reality under any circumstance—may your wife be in China!—you are quite mistaken." She eyed him with disgust, shaking her head at the incongruity of his blond good looks and the villainy of his nature. "Sarah would probably be better off without you," she mused aloud. Her finger caressed the trigger.

"Consider her delicate condition. She has but just recently been delivered of a child, Kitty," Benjamin faltered, his voice rising a pitch as his nervousness increased.

Until that moment, Benjamin's aggressive stance had surprised and baffled Kitty. His high opinion of himself had evidently sustained him in his daring attempt at seduction, despite his obvious fear. But now he was beginning to show signs of indecisiveness.

She imagined he was loath to back down now when the quarry he had been assiduously stalking for the past month was so nearly his. But surely he would not risk his life to complete his conquest. That thought gave her courage.

"I had hoped to leave without it coming to this, Benjamin," she said, her voice more controlled now. "But you go too far. When I discovered the key to my bedchamber door had somehow been misplaced this afternoon, I suspected your part in the charade. I therefore took precautions." She tossed back the strands of raven hair that had fallen across her forehead and indicated her gun with a curt nod.

Benjamin seemed to consider for a moment and, blinking through the perspiration that dripped from his brow, suggested, "You would not kill me, Kitty. I am your cousin."

Kitty could not answer at first. She bit her lip, pondering her response. He was right; she couldn't kill him.

"No, I will not kill you," she agreed finally in a quiet, measured tone.

Benjamin stepped forward, the beginnings of a self-satisfied smile curving his finely molded lips.

"But I have no compunction about shooting you," she continued, lowering her gun several inches and aiming at a very different part of his body. "And where you would least like it."

Of a naturally pale countenance, Benjamin turned a most unearthly shade of white. He trembled visibly, though he stood his ground, much as a spoiled, sullen child who has been denied a coveted gooseberry tart but is unwilling to forgo the pleasure despite the certainty of punishment.

Oh, how she wished he were still in Northumberland and her father were still alive! Why had Papa left her so dependent on this hideous excuse for a man? Kitty forced back the sting of tears and reminded herself fiercely that the entailment laws overrode whatever wishes her father might have had concerning her. And Papa hadn't known that Benjamin was such a beast—they hadn't seen him since his boyhood. If he'd known Benjamin's character, perhaps he'd have managed to make some provision for her somehow....

"You and your precious virginity!"

Kitty's thoughts were abruptly interrupted by the distasteful object of them.

"You may leave this house and take your virginity with you quite unsullied, for all I care," he spat disparagingly, flinging out his arms to show his final, angry capitulation.

"I intend to," she replied, her head rising haughtily and her heart singing with relief and triumph. "For even if I did wish to give it away, it would not be to the likes of you. Get out!"

Benjamin withdrew to the door, muttering crude expletives and throwing a hate-filled glare over his broad, retreating shoulders. With his hand on the knob, he could not refrain from a last sour remark, ground out between clenched teeth. "You are probably not worth the effort, Kitty."

"You will never know, Benjamin!" came the sweet reply.

"WHERE CAN THE GIRL BE? I sent the carriage for her more than two hours ago!" exclaimed Lady Dinwiddie. She looked impatiently out her second-storey sitting-room window into the gathering dusk of a late July evening.

As she leaned over the windowsill the last rays of the setting sun touched her silver hair and gave it a soft, rosy glow to match the raspberry-coloured ribbons that adorned her sarsnet gown. The colour became her and added charm to her round, surprisingly unlined face.

"It has been but an hour, my dear," soothed her husband, who stood just inside the door with a copy of the *Gazette* tucked into the crook of his arm. He loved his wife and was a little bemused by the radiant picture she presented, but shook his head to recover his presence of mind and continued. "I just wanted you to know I will be in the library."

"Ah, the poor child," sighed Lady Dinwiddie, unconsciously though quite effectively ignoring her husband. "To lose her mother at such an early age, and now her papa!"

"Yes, they were uncommonly attached. More so than usual between a father and his daughter. But then Whitchurch had no sons," he observed, turning to go.

"Too attached, I say!" began Lady Dinwiddie.

A massive man with a thick head of grey hair and an intelligent, good-humoured countenance, Lord Dinwiddie turned again to patiently attend his wife as she pursued her favourite and most absorbing subject.

"He was too lenient with the girl!" she continued, pacing the splendid Aubusson rug that covered the floor and twisting a lace-edged handkerchief in her small, plump hands. "Though he secured her an excellent education and had her instructed in all the social graces, she has never had the opportunity to put her accomplishments to the test! For why ever else would a girl want accomplishments except to please a man?" Lady Dinwiddie looked to Lord Dinwiddie for affirmation of this irrefutable fact. He raised his brows and opened his mouth to hazard a differing opinion, but Lady Dinwiddie rushed on, "I begged leave of him many times to permit me to arrange Katherine's proper entrée into Society. As her godmother it is my responsibility! But she would not leave her father for a season in town, nor even for a short stay here at Ridley Hall. And Thomas Whitchurch would not insist on anything that did not precisely suit her!''

As it was obvious to his lordship that his wife intended to vent her feelings, he sat down in the nearest chair and obligingly contributed. ''I am surprised that she wishes to make a stay with us now. She seemed determined to stay at Whitchurch when we broached the subject with her directly following the funeral. Then, when Benjamin arrived and insisted she remain in what had always been her home, she eagerly acquiesced. I wonder what has occurred to make her change her mind?''

''No doubt seeing her cousin and his wife so happily wed and with a newborn child has made her more inclined to seek an establishment of her own. She is, after all, going on twenty years of age, Arthur, and will be on the shelf if she is not careful! I could not bear to see my lovely goddaughter playing nanny to a tribe of little ruffians belonging to her cousin, bowing and scraping to their every wish, just so she might show her gratitude for residing in their home!''

''I do not anticipate such an ignominious fate for Katherine.'' Lord Dinwiddie chuckled. ''Rest easy, my dear. You cannot fail to establish the child. And even if you do not find her a suitable husband, with four or five thousand a year, and she were obliged to return to Whitchurch House, I cannot imagine Katherine Whitchurch bowing and scraping to anyone!''

"Arthur, despite your sanguine attitude I must predict—" Diverted by the sound of an approaching carriage, Lady Dinwiddie moved eagerly to the window. "Oh, here she is now! She is just turning in at the gate. I must go down. I will bring her to you in the drawing room. Make haste, my love!"

Lord Dinwiddie followed his wife out of the room and down the stairs to the drawing room at the slow, comfortable pace he judged more conducive to minimizing stress on his aging joints than the helter-skelter way in which his lady larked about.

If Kitty had been at all worried about her reception, she would have been put immediately at ease by the spectacle of Lady Dinwiddie waving enthusiastically from the flagged stone steps of Ridley Hall. Though her ladyship had found occasion in the past to remonstrate with her goddaughter for conduct she deemed unsuitable in a young lady of breeding, her affection for the girl could not be denied. Almost the minute Kitty stepped out the door of the carriage she received a warm embrace and a light peck on the cheek from her godmother. Since she was of taller than average height and Lady Dinwiddie rather short, this was not an easy task.

The affectionate exchange was further thwarted by the plump bundle of fur Kitty held in her arms. Cleopatra heartily resented the crush and indicated her discomfort with a loud hiss of disapproval.

"Oh!" exclaimed Lady Dinwiddie, quickly stepping back and bumping into a startled footman. "I did not observe at first that you had brought your...animal."

"Forgive Cleopatra, Godmama," said Kitty, laughing easily and setting her disgruntled pet on the ground. "She is not dangerous, as you must know, but is a decidedly jealous creature. I've brought my horse, too." She motioned to the chestnut mare tethered to the back of the carriage. "You don't mind, do you?"

"Heavens, no, I do not mind...I suppose. Come, dear." Lady Dinwiddie turned to the austere-looking butler standing stiffly at the top of the steps, and in an effort to recover some of her dignity, said in a haughty tone wholly unlike herself, "See to the horse, please, Hiller."

Hiller had long since become accustomed to Lady Dinwiddie and merely bowed respectfully. A footman had already been dispatched to the stables for just that purpose.

Moments later the two women entered the drawing room, followed closely by Cleopatra. Lord Dinwiddie turned from the table where he was pouring himself a brandy and watched Kitty cross the large salon to where he stood.

She wore an old dress which he could see she had outgrown, for the thin material pulled taut over her bosom and came a little short at the ankle. But even the faded blue muslin could not detract from the loveliness of her person. Tall and slender, with a mass of ebony hair piled carelessly atop her head, finely textured skin and animated green eyes flecked with gold, she could not help but be admired.

"Good evening, Katherine, and welcome," he said, taking both her hands in his. "As you are my near neighbour's daughter and my wife's godchild, I have seen you on numerous occasions since you were in leading strings, but I confess I had not realized until now how lovely and grown up you have become."

Kitty smiled unselfconsciously and teasingly rejoined, "What a disarming speech, my lord. But doing it a bit brown, aren't you? And please call me Kitty! Katherine is so ponderous. I only hope I will not prove to be too great a nuisance to you."

"Nonsense, Katherine," said Lady Dinwiddie, who had never been able to bring herself to call her goddaughter Kitty. "As you well know, I would have had you with us much sooner had my wishes been attended to. I have always wanted a daughter, and as your godmother, Katherine, I hope you will allow me certain privileges that would have belonged to your dear mama. I have plans for you, my dear—" Here she suddenly cut herself short and hastily exclaimed, "Oh, but let us sit down! That may all be discussed at a later date."

Everyone was at last seated and Cleopatra serenely claimed her mistress's lap. Kitty had noted Lady Dinwiddie's nervousness with some amusement and said, "If those plans mean you wish to put me in the way of acquiring a husband, Godmama, rest assured I mean to cooperate. You see, I have finally concluded there is no other recourse for me. I would have happily lived with Papa into ancient spinsterhood, but he is gone now, and I find I cannot bear the thought of becoming a governess shackled to a group of obdurate children, or a lady's companion enduring the whims of a demanding mistress.'' She smiled impishly. ''I own I should prefer marriage to those alternatives.''

Lady Dinwiddie was so overcome by Kitty's revelations that speech was temporarily beyond her, while Lord Dinwiddie was much diverted by her businesslike attitude. Most girls her age could not discuss such a subject without a great deal of embarrassment or affectation, punctuated by simpers or giggles. Kitty did not seem in the least encumbered by romantic notions of any variety.

''Forgive me if I overstep the bounds of our friendship, my dear,'' began Lord Dinwiddie, ''but as I was not required at the reading of your father's will I do not precisely understand the terms. Naturally your cousin received the estate, I know, but did your father leave you no income at all?''

''Why, dearest, you know Thomas Whitchurch never had a feather to fly with....''

Lord Dinwiddie silenced his wife's untactful outburst with a quelling glance, but Kitty only laughed.

''Never mind, Lord Dinwiddie, we all know it is the truth.'' Her smile vanished, however, and she continued on a more pensive note. ''He meant to provide for me eventually, I'm sure, because he knew the small portion left to me by my mother could never provide me with an independence. 'Tis good only for pin money, I'm afraid," she added ruefully.

"But you were welcome to stay at Whitchurch, were you not, Kitty? You come to us, I hope, of your own accord?" questioned Lord Dinwiddie, his keen eyes narrowing almost imperceptibly.

"Yes, of course. I was certainly welcome there, and I believe cousin Benjamin saw me go with some...regret," answered Kitty, returning Lord Dinwiddie's gaze unwaveringly. "But to be perfectly honest, my lord, Benjamin and I did not rub along well together. He found me to be stubborn on occasion." She hastened to add with a sweet, docile smile, "But I shall be most biddable here, I promise."

"Well, we shall soon see how you like my plans," said Lady Dinwiddie, delighted by Kitty's unexpected complaisance, "because in less than a fortnight we are expecting my sister and my niece, Agatha, from London, and with them a small party of friends. And of course, Agatha's fiancé, Nathan Alexander, Earl of Hatherleigh." This last was said with considerable emphasis and pride, as if the name should provoke some response. When it did not, she went on.

"They will remain two or three weeks and it will be a perfect opportunity for you to become familiar with elegant society before a season in town. That is, of course, if I can prevail upon you to go!''

"I look forward to seeing Agatha again," Kitty responded politely, adroitly sidestepping her god-mother's reference to a London season. "I rode with her quite a bit the summer she spent with you—was it two years ago? I imagine her mother has been busy making quite sure Agatha's future is secure. And obviously, if Agatha is engaged, her mother did well."

"'Did well' is rather a tame expression in this case," declared Lady Dinwiddie with a wave of her handkerchief and a decided nod of her head. "To acquire Hatherleigh as a son-in-law is a major feat! He is wealthy and extremely presentable. Travels in the first circles, you know! He has only recently in-herited and I imagine feels it requisite that he pro-duce an heir. He certainly did not appear disposed to marriage at all until recently."

"Agatha is very beautiful," Kitty said matter-of-factly.

"True, and though your beauty is of a different kind than dear Agatha's and your fortune clearly unremarkable..." began Lady Dinwiddie.

"You mean clearly nonexistent, don't you, God-mama?" interjected Kitty with a teasing smile.

"...you might do well in the marriage mart if managed properly," concluded Lady Dinwiddie, pointedly ignoring the interruption. "It is fortunate that your father was so adamant that you were not to wear black upon his death and for the usual year afterward. I abhor the practice! Most women, myself included, look ghastly in such a melancholy hue."

"I shall take care not to die then, my dear," murmured his lordship from behind the folds of his newspaper where he had taken refuge when the conversation had begun to lose interest for him.

"It was just like Papa to relieve me of an observance that would continually remind me of my loss," said Kitty thoughtfully. "But I cannot help honouring his memory in small ways." She gently touched the black ribbon that secured her bonnet.

"Well, two weeks should be just enough time for my dressmaker to make up several gowns," Lady Dinwiddie cheerfully interjected. "Not in bright colours, of course, but suitable at least for our present purposes. When, er, if we go to London, I will take you to Madame Signoret on Bond Street. Now, my dear, I'll show you to your room. There is no need to call Mrs. Wells. We need not stand upon ceremony!"

Kitty took leave of Lord Dinwiddie and followed her new guardian up the wide, handsome staircase to the upper floor.

When the ladies reached Kitty's bedchamber they found her abigail, Leah, just hanging the last of her few gowns in the wardrobe. Lady Dinwiddie took the opportunity to look through the meagre collection and note what her goddaughter needed. To her consternation, she found that Kitty had not a single suitable garment. Upon further perusal she found the patched and mended underthings to be sadly lacking, as well.

"Kitty, though you did not entertain, I cannot understand your not taking the trouble to dress properly!" Lady Dinwiddie exclaimed, clucking distastefully over a limp, threadbare chemise.

"Papa never noticed what I wore," Kitty replied gently. "And I had rather spend whatever money I could spare from the household for a new book, for as you know, I had much rather learn about the Egyptian civilization than have a new gown."

"Well, I hope you are not such a bluestocking that you will put off the gentlemen," sniffed Lady Dinwiddie. She refolded several pieces of clothing she had inspected and summarily thrown on the bed before continuing. "Much can be attributed to your lack of a mother, but now that you are of an age and inclined to marry, you must dress and act the proper young lady! It is fortunate that Agatha is to come, because she is the perfect example for you to emulate. Such pretty manners, such a dainty carriage, such a lilting, feminine tone of voice..."

An involuntary twitch of Kitty's mouth, followed by a definite grimace was only partially seen by Lady Dinwiddie. But it was enough.

"My dear, such a face! Whatever is the matter with you?"

"Oh . . . it was just a slight pain," she declared, laying her hand just beneath the fullness of her breasts. "It must be Cook's turnip omelette I had for lunch."

"Turnip omelette! It sounds perfectly odious! Was it a new recipe?"

"Yes," said Kitty, her eyes wide and ingenuous. "As I am blessed with a healthy appetite she often tries them out on me. I cannot blame her. Our harvest of turnips this year is prodigious."

"Perhaps our cook should prepare an herbal tea to purge you of the noxious substance," her ladyship suggested, her brows puckering in concern.

"Oh, that is not necessary," Kitty hastily reassured her. "It has passed."

"But I insist that you get into a nightdress and retire early, Katherine. I will make your excuses to Lord Dinwiddie at dinner. You have had a lot to deal with of late, my girl, and I do not wish you to go into a decline just when I have got you where I want you! But dear, where are your nightdresses?" She had been looking about the pieces of clothing during this last speech and now turned questioning eyes to her goddaughter.

"Can you not find them?" asked Kitty, flushing slightly and producing a short, nervous laugh. "Leah must have forgotten to pack them."

Leah did not deign to notice the comment but continued to put things away.

"It does not signify," said Lady Dinwiddie. "They probably need to be replaced, as well. You may wear one of mine. It will be sadly short, but will do for tonight."

She left the room and returned within minutes with a long-sleeved, high-necked, pink cambric gown festooned with numerous flounces and furbelows and closed in the back by at least twenty tiny pearl buttons.

Kitty could hardly imagine taking the trouble to get into this atrocity, much less sleeping in it. She thanked Lady Dinwiddie nonetheless, and with Leah's help disrobed and struggled into it, choking back her amusement when she saw herself reflected in the mirror above the dressing table.

"Except for the length," said Lady Dinwiddie, looking down at Kitty's shapely legs sticking out a good ten inches from the scalloped hem, "it is altogether charming. I'll have just such another made up for you, my dear."

Kitty found herself quite speechless.

Lady Dinwiddie finally made to go, promising not to pay her another visit to fuss over her if Kitty intended to go right to sleep. Already propped up against the pillows on her bed, and pulling out the pins that held up her hair, Kitty assured her that she would. Lady Dinwiddie left the room.

Leah remained behind and composedly inquired if Kitty wished her to brush out and braid her hair.

"Pray, do not make me hysterical, Leah," she said with a laugh, swinging her legs over the side of the bed and standing up. "You may brush out my hair, but you know I do not braid it at night, nor do I wear nightdresses like this that surely resemble the restraining gowns they use at Bedlam!"

She turned her back to the middle-aged plump servant who was now smiling, and pulled her thick, waving tresses of hair into a haphazard pile atop her head, so it would be out of the way. "But first help me out of this, please! And do forgive me for blaming the absence of my nightdresses on your neglect, Leah. I do not think Godmama would understand my passion for sleeping in Papa's nightshirts. You did bring one, didn't you?"

"Under your pillow, miss," Leah replied with a tolerant, affectionate shake of her head.

"Godmama is very proper, isn't she, Leah?" said Kitty, speaking with the freedom and candour she had always employed with her abigail.

"To be sure, miss," said Leah ominously. "Her ladyship is most proper."

"And I, too, shall be most proper," said Kitty in a determined tone, "if that is what I must do to procure a husband."

Leah merely pursed her lips.

"Well," said Kitty, turning and observing that look of disbelief, "I shall try at least to appear most proper when there are others about!"

CHAPTER TWO

KITTY'S BODY moved with the horse, plunging with invigorating momentum into every dip and bounding lightly over every swell in the open, uncultivated fields of Lord Dinwiddie's estate. The stars had dimmed and the first light of dawn was quickly banishing the last of the deep purple night.

Clothed in breeches and a schoolboy's small tailored jacket, she was free to straddle her horse and abandon all thoughts of propriety for a robust gallop through the countryside. Since she was unencumbered by the skirts of a riding habit and had shoved her long hair into a tight cap, she looked and rode like a young man.

A short summer cloudburst, the kind that begins quite suddenly and departs just as suddenly, had left the foliage dappled with drops of rain and the air full of the smell of wet earth. She felt she could ride forever. But mindful of her horse and anxious that she should not work the young chestnut mare beyond endurance, she slowed to a halt near a stream and dismounted.

"There Jezebel, off you go," she said, patting the velvety haunches of her horse. "Drink and rest a bit, then we must get back."

She was on a small hill just above the road that carried post coaches between the moderate-sized town of Trumpington and the village of Barley, and thence on to London. She had an expansive view of Lord Dinwiddie's considerable property, which began just on the other side of the road. There was Ridley Hall, dark and quiet, the servants just beginning to stir.

Kitty was feeling a slight pricking of her conscience for eluding her guardians, but she had been extremely good for the past several days. She had stood long and patiently whilst the dressmaker had pinned her into endless gowns, nightdresses, morning gowns, walking gowns, ball gowns... She felt she deserved to ride off her fidgets in a burst of freedom. Lady Dinwiddie would not understand, and it was best, therefore, she did not know.

Kitty calculated that she had perhaps half an hour left before the servants would be about above stairs, so she must return now to avoid exposure. As she rose, a sound below drew her attention, and by the growing light she discerned a rider on the Trumpington road. It was a tall figure—a man, she concluded, in a most relaxed attitude atop his horse. The muted clop-clop of the horse's hooves echoed in the silent morning. It was a handsome horse, she observed, well appointed and of the purest white.

Except for her appreciation of the horse, the scene held no interest for her beyond a momentary visual diversion. But she could not help wondering if the gentleman—if gentleman he were—had been visiting the Duck and Dog Inn. The establishment was notorious in the area for its gaming activities and the light skirts who peddled their wares between duties as bar and scullery maids. As a gentlewoman, she knew she had no business even knowing of its existence, but she had often been privy to the unguarded conversations of the stable boys at Whitchurch. They had grown so used to her presence that they did not always realize she was in earshot of their scandalous disclosures.

Her speculations, however, were soon ended. The sounds of fast-moving vehicles and slurred, drunken commands of "Out of the way, curse you! Over, damn you, pull over!" abruptly cut through the stillness and ended the rider's leisurely perambulation. He jerked his head around and observed, as did Kitty, two high-perch phaetons careering down the road at a perilous speed.

Hastily he turned his horse's leads to the right, but the horse was frightened by the unexpected commotion and reared up to an astonishing height. Kitty stood aghast, fearful that the horse would throw its master directly under the thundering hooves of the approaching horses.

The phaetons were upon him. Kitty closed her eyes in fear of witnessing the most dreadful accident. In another moment they had passed, but even as the noise they created became more and more distant, Kitty was afraid to look. Had the man been trampled to death?

"Damn! Who the devil...? Hell to pay if ever I find out...! Racing on this road at this damnable hour!"

Kitty's eyes flew open at the first oath. She swayed in relief. Thank God the man was not dead! She could just see him through a cloud of dust, struggling to his feet from the midst of the sturdy gorse bushes that lined the road.

He brushed at his coat sleeves in evident disgust and gingerly turned and flexed each arm and leg as if testing them. He appeared to have survived the horrendous episode without injury. But where was his horse? Ah, there it was, just coming out from beneath the shade of a nearby oak. It was evidently still quite nervous and skittish, for though the man approached carefully, speaking in a low, soothing lilt, the horse pranced around in an agitated manner and finally reared up again, its pale flanks gleaming in the early light. Then, with one last dismayed whinny, it turned and galloped down the road toward Barley.

To Kitty's consternation, Jezebel, until then as quiet an onlooker as herself, responded to the other horse's plight with a whinny of her own.

Instantly the man jerked his head in their direction and Kitty could not avoid being seen.

"Lad, come here! Do you wish to earn a shilling for little effort?" Kitty did not move. "Don't dawdle, fellow!" the man cried impatiently. "Come and be useful. There has been a mishap here!"

Perhaps because of an innate curiosity or perhaps because the gentleman had such an air of authority in his tone, Kitty took Jezebel by the reins and led her down the incline, stopping within a few feet of the stranger. He was a gentleman, a little disheveled and rumpled looking at the moment, but his clothing was fine and well tailored, displaying his tall, straight figure to advantage. He was bare-headed, and his hair looked almost blue black in the luminescent rays of the rising sun.

"Where is it you live, young man?" asked the gentleman, still intent on brushing the dirt from his breeches.

"In...in Barley, sir." It was all she could think of to say.

"Good! I can only guess why a young lad like yourself is out at this extraordinary hour, but I imagine you ought to get home before you are got into trouble. Carry me with you into Barley and I'll pay you a shilling."

Kitty cursed her slowness of wit. Why hadn't she said she lived in Trumpington, the town he had just left?

"What about your horse, sir?" she stalled.

"So you saw the whole thing, did you? Well, you must have seen then that Lightning has bolted and is well on his way to Barley. He's a bit skittish, but quite intelligent. He'll probably return to the Black Swan, where I'm staying. Or perhaps we might catch up with him on the road. Either way we'd best be going."

Kitty was in a quandary. Under other circumstances she would have been quite willing to assist the gentleman, but she could not waste another moment before she returned to Ridley. The pink light of dawn was flooding the surrounding fields. Travelling on horse into Barley would be much more expeditious for the gentleman, certainly, but he would have to walk.

"I'm sorry, sir," said Kitty. "But I cannot help you."

"What?" The gentleman's look and tone were incredulous. "I can hardly credit any young man would not appreciate a shilling so easily acquired. You say you are going to Barley anyway, so..."

The gentleman had not previously looked closely at Kitty. He did so now. Large eyes, whose precise colour had been indeterminable in the half light, dominated a slender face that seemed finely boned for a boy whose height declared him to be in his teens.

A strange expression flitted over the man's face. Kitty could not interpret it and that made her nervous. Feeling a sudden panic, she turned quickly, but the pivot allowed the gentleman to observe the womanly swell of her buttocks, insufficiently hidden by the short length of the boy's jacket. Hers were not the hips of a boy!

With a smooth, swift movement he stepped forward, clasped Kitty by her wrist and swung her around with one hand, pulling off her cap with the other. Kitty dropped Jezebel's reins, and an astonished gasp escaped her as her hair tumbled in unruly profusion to the middle of her back.

"Good Lord, you *are* a girl! An extremely lovely one, too." He cocked his head, frowned as if considering a puzzle, then suddenly smiled. "Is it possible? Could that greedy old innkeeper have sent you after me, even though I told him I do not consort with barmaids of such very indiscriminate habits? But why else would such an alluring bit of fluff be dressed thus and found so alone on a country road? You are lovely...."

Utterly confused at first, Kitty suddenly realized the import of his words. Indignation swelled in her chest, and she opened her mouth to deny such an offensive idea and to put this impudent fellow in his place. But before she could speak, she found herself ruthlessly pulled against the gentleman's chest and securely held there by a firm arm around her waist and a strong hand pressed against the back of her neck. She looked at him in complete disbelief as he lowered first his smiling gaze, and then his mouth to hers.

The kiss was over quickly, but when the gentleman raised his head and looked into her eyes, Kitty found it difficult to focus.

She knew she ought to be struggling furiously to free herself from this stranger, but she had a most humiliating inclination to taste the warm, brandied pressure of his lips against hers again. His mouth curved into another wickedly attractive smile.

"What a strange little wench you are," he said wonderingly. "You kiss as though you've never been kissed before." His smile suddenly took on a more cynical slant. "But then I'm sure men pay your innkeeper plenty for such a treat. I, however tempted I am, will not indulge myself with such false pleasures. You are *too* like an innocent for me!" He released her.

Kitty's knees buckled alarmingly when he released her, but she willed strength into her sagging limbs and stood stiffly before him. "I am a gentleman's daughter! I am not acquainted with this innkeeper you speak of! You have no right to speak so to me!" She wasn't sure what made her angrier: his casual assumption that she was a light skirt, or her own weak, stupid reaction to his kiss. Such confusion was lowering and she could feel her face flushing with shame.

"No proper young lady," he said coolly, as he resumed the vain attempt to dust his breeches, "rides about in such a hoydenish fashion."

Kitty knew she could not reveal who she was. She did not wish her godmother and Lord Dinwiddie to become the subject of gossip. That would be a poor return for all their kindness, and after all, she had brought this whole thing on herself by doing precisely what they would not wish her to do.

But it rankled to be so lightly dismissed by this man. Wasn't there something she could do to prove to him that she was not the fallen woman he supposed her to be? Then it occurred to her that she should be outraged by his kissing her, that she should . . . yes! She should slap his face!

"What? You're still here?" he enquired as he straightened up from the task of arranging his disordered clothing. "Hadn't you best get back to the inn before you have wasted any more of your time and your keeper's money?"

If Kitty had been undecided before, this sneering comment was the last straw. She raised her hand and brought her open palm squarely towards his jaw. His reflexes were excellent and he caught her hand just before it made contact, the hard pressure of his grip around her wrist surprising her so that her fingers curled. Instead of slapping him soundly, she unintentionally scraped him with her fingernails, grown fashionably long at Lady Dinwiddie's urging. At his involuntary grunt of pain, Kitty's heart leaped in sympathy and remorse.

"Now look what you've made me do!" she cried. "If you'd only stood still like a gentleman!"

"My girl, you are the outside of enough!" exclaimed the man with amused exasperation, pulling a handkerchief from his pocket and dabbing at his jaw, which was now producing tiny beads of blood. "Why should I stand stock-still and allow myself to be pummeled by a chit like you merely because—"

"Because you kissed me, you, you...loathsome libertine!" Kitty was proud to have come up with such an apt description of the gentleman's character. She stood taller and glared at him disdainfully.

"And you did not wish it?" he inquired mockingly.

"Why should you think I wished it?" she retorted, wiping her hand fiercely across her mouth to accentuate her point.

"I see a young woman standing by the road, quite alone, in the wee small hours of the morning—"

"And you stupidly assume—"

"Dressed thus..." he continued, ignoring her heated interruption. He waved his free hand towards her figure, his eyes following the curve of her waist and slender thighs. He looked away suddenly, rubbing his fingers between his eyebrows in obvious agitation. "I wonder I did not observe your womanhood upon first encountering you," he said in a lowered voice. "The light and my concern for the horse must account for it."

"It seems you quite forgot your horse just now!" Kitty broke in.

"Despite your appearance," he continued, "you do speak with the tone of a gentlewoman. But I've met many a bit o'muslin that has been well taught not to abuse the King's English. I do not know what you are...or what your game is." He cast her a look that was both dark and perplexed. "But it does not signify. I'm tired and I wish to go to bed." He started to turn away but stopped and raised a brow, his lips stretching into a slight grimace Kitty thought he must have meant as a smile. "Alone."

Words would not come to Kitty as she stood watching him, rubbing the wrist he had held in such an iron grasp. He turned and strode in an unhurried manner down the road towards Barley. She stared after him, wishing passionately for the courage to hurl a rock at his head. But she was already remorseful for drawing blood on his face, and she was dismally aware that rendering him unconscious would make her feel even more miserable. If only she could think of something devastating to say, but she was nonplussed by the complete self-composure this gentleman seemed to possess.

The brightening light of day recalled her to the immediate necessity of a hasty return to Ridley. With one last glare at the gentleman, who did not deign to turn again to look at her, she rode off in the opposite direction and entered into Lord Dinwiddie's grounds by a circuitous route. This she did in case, however unlikely, she was being watched.

"MY LOVE, you look absolutely charming," effused Lady Dinwiddie when Kitty walked into her ladyship's sitting room just as the mantel clock struck eleven. "I was not thoroughly persuaded when Miss Beaufort first showed us the pattern sketches for your new gowns. They seemed decidedly plain to *me*. But on you, Katherine, they are absolutely chic!"

Miss Beaufort had been Lady Dinwiddie's country dressmaker for several years and had designed an endless assortment of outrageous outfits for her. Lady Dinwiddie insisted on profusely detailed gowns on the principle that if some were good, more was better. Her ladyship had already been long set in her ways before the talented dressmaker had become known to her, and Miss Beaufort had given up on ever changing the tastes of her noble patroness. But when the elegantly proportioned Miss Whitchurch was produced and an entire wardrobe commissioned, the seamstress was ecstatic at the opportunity. She pressed urgently, ultimately successfully, for permission to create a different style altogether for Lady Dinwiddie's new ward.

"I own I do find this gown becoming," said Kitty, smoothing the material of her summer gown with its decided Grecian lines. The muslin was a delicate, seafoam green, sprigged with yellow daisies, and the combination of colours flattered her eyes to perfection.

"And your hair is vastly improved. Less severe than before!" Lady Dinwiddie added, eyeing Kitty's dark tresses piled into a fetching style with curling tendrils falling delicately onto her high brow. "There are two eligible gentlemen attending my sister and Agatha, and I dare predict a conquest for you, my dear! I do hope you will not dismiss Cedric Cranfield if he pays you some attention, Katherine, even though you may think him a bit of a prig!"

"Who is Mr. Cranfield?" asked Kitty, sitting down in a blue satin wing chair and positioning her hands just so in her lap.

"Oh, did I not tell you who was to be of the party? That was remiss of me, but I have been so preoccupied with the arrangements and all. I did tell you Agatha's father died, didn't I?"

Kitty nodded. "Some time ago, was it not?"

"It has been eighteen months, I believe. Well, after mourning her husband in black gloves for a decent year's interval, my sister remarried a widower of some means—Viscount Cranfield by title. Cedric is the youngest of his three sons by his first marriage but will have a profitable family living upon the death of a certain aged clergyman in Essex. His great-uncle, I think. His father, Cedric's, that is, died within a se'nnight following the nuptials! Can you imagine! And so my poor sister is once more draped in black. But it does not signify, because she retains the title, and since she is as rich as a nabob she will not miss the income that now falls to the new viscount, Cedric's eldest brother, Andrew."

"So Cedric is Agatha's stepbrother," Kitty concluded with a teasing smile.

"Yes, and so I should have said in the beginning," chuckled Lady Dinwiddie. "Sir William Stonebridge is the other gentleman to whom I referred. He was a close friend of the late Viscount Cranfield, and my sister, in a manner of speaking, inherited him upon her husband's demise. He was, and still is, a frequent guest at the Cranfield town house. The new viscount chooses to rusticate year round in the country and has quite given over the town house for my sister's use. Isn't that kind of him?"

"Indeed," Kitty murmured.

"And, by the by, Katherine, Sir William is extremely wealthy, and therefore an even more desirable possibility for you. He has money, so he does not need to marry for it. He already did that, I assure you. His first wife left his pockets well-lined indeed, but he has remained a widower these fifteen years, at least. People say that though he may flirt outrageously he will never marry again." She stood up and walked to the window.

"Do you expect them already, Godmama?"

"I do hope they arrive soon. Lord Dinwiddie says I can never wait patiently and quietly for an expected visitor, and I suppose he is right. But I fear for them all when it comes to travelling these treacherous out-of-the-way roads where highwaymen are most apt to be encountered. They pass through Pultney Heath, you know."

"Surely they do not travel at night?" questioned Kitty.

"No. They were to stay one night in Tilbury, and then were to arise early and travel on to Barley to meet Lord Hatherleigh at the posting inn there," she said, peering down the London road as far as she could see.

A disquieting thought had just entered Kitty's brain, and she felt her muscles tense involuntarily. "Then the earl did not travel with them from London?"

"He left London several days ago to attend to business on one of his estates and made plans to meet them at the Black Swan. Since they could not calculate the exact time of their arrival, Lord Hatherleigh chose to meet them there. He did not wish to presume upon my hospitality and told Agatha that he had rather wait for her."

It would be hideous and indeed an unlikely coincidence but Kitty pressed on, assuming an air of polite curiosity. "Oh, then you have never been introduced to the earl? You've never seen him?"

"On the contrary, Katherine, we've met on numerous occasions. But even if we had not been formally introduced, he is hardly a man to be lost in the crowd. I remember the first time I saw him, his head perhaps three inches above the . . ."

Kitty leaned forward ever so slightly in her chair, but was disappointed in her wish to hear a description of Lord Hatherleigh when Lady Dinwiddie abruptly exclaimed, "Oh, there they are at last! Three carriages altogether! Come, Kitty, come!"

Kitty was bustled downstairs and into the drawing room and made to wait in dignified state until their elegant guests had alighted from the carriages and entered the house. As though they had not been expecting visitors at all, Lady Dinwiddie and Kitty sat down and arranged their skirts. They were just in time, for now they heard voices and footsteps in the hall, and then a high-pitched girlish laugh Kitty remembered from two years ago.

Agatha and Lady Cranfield entered the room, arm in arm, and Agatha seemed to be enjoying something her mother was whispering to her. Her pale and elaborately coiffed head was thrown back in laughter, exposing the beautiful, slender lines of her neck. She was even smaller than Kitty remembered and much lovelier. Her complexion was pink-and-white perfection, her figure light and graceful and her travelling dress a powder-blue vision of Bond Street elegance.

Upon perceiving her aunt standing to greet them, Agatha abruptly disengaged herself from her mama and rushed with arms outstretched. "Aunt Louisa, my dearest creature! It's been an age!"

"La, child, so it has!" concurred Lady Dinwiddie, embracing her niece. Then she extended her hand to Lady Cranfield. "And sister dear, I believe it is even longer since I have seen you!"

"Louisa, it has been too, too long!" agreed Lady Cranfield, waddling forward in a voluminous black silk to receive her share of affectionate greetings. Kitty could not help but stare at Lady Cranfield, whom she had never seen before. She was finding it very difficult to believe that such a ponderously large mother had bred the fairylike Agatha.

"And here is my dearest of friends, Miss Theresa Bidwell," Agatha was now saying, as she drew a tall, rather plain young woman into the circle of women. Miss Bidwell looked quite shy and nearly overcome by the exuberant reception from the good-natured, demonstrative Lady Dinwiddie.

The scene, whether sincere or affected she could not ascertain, fascinated Kitty. She was not used to social fal-de-ral, and in any case the four ladies stood directly in front of her and so close to her chair that she could not stand up. She had been so bemused by the spectacle of Lady Cranfield and the lovely Agatha when they first entered the room, that she had quite forgotten the necessity of standing up to receive them, and Lady Dinwiddie had apparently forgotten her existence. She could hear masculine voices behind the group of women, but it was some time before the effusive Lady Dinwiddie recovered sufficiently to step aside and introduce her new ward.

"But of course I remember dear Kitty," cried Agatha when the latter could at last gratefully stand up. "We had a charming time together the summer before my first season in London! We are changed greatly, are we not?" Another tinkling laugh. "And now you must see the results of my second season in town, Kitty. This is my fiancé, Nathan Alexander, Earl of Hatherleigh!"

At last Kitty was allowed to see past their little circle to observe the other guests. They had been conversing with Lord Dinwiddie, who had luckily come into the room at the precise moment to keep them from being rather rudely ignored by his distracted, overexcited wife.

A tall gentleman, impeccably dressed in a jacket of rich green superfine, champagne-coloured pantaloons and Hessians polished to a reflective brilliance, stood with his back to them, but turned when Agatha laid her tiny hand on his arm. The black hair and wide, muscular expanse of his shoulders were all too familiar. Kitty felt a sudden sickening lurch in her stomach and had a frantic desire to flee. But she hid her feelings behind a polite smile and stood her ground.

"Nathan, my love, I wish you to meet an old friend of mine. This is Miss Katherine Whitchurch, but we call her Kitty! She is my dear aunt's godchild and is come to stay with them!"

Kitty's worst fears were realized. When the gentleman turned around she looked into that same face she had first seen only hours earlier and had hoped never to behold again. The finely chiseled, aristocratic features could be clearly seen now in the unflinching light of full day. A placid—or was it bored?—expression immediately fled his countenance and was replaced by one of simple surprise. His eyebrows shot up so far that Kitty felt his reaction could not possibly go unremarked.

"Why, Nathan, you are staring most rudely at my friend!" admonished Agatha, hanging on his arm possessively and gazing up at him with a pout on her small, piquant face.

"It is only that I thought for a brief moment that I had met your friend before," said Lord Hatherleigh, recollecting himself. "But I can see now that I was mistaken. I am pleased to make your acquaintance, Miss Whitchurch," he concluded suavely, bowing gracefully over the hand she had most reluctantly given him.

She managed to maintain her rather frozen smile, though she felt a pang when she saw the thin red marks her nails had made on his manly jaw. She tried to keep her eyes from straying to that particular part of his face and wondered how he had explained his injury. She felt him looking at her and experienced a strange chill travel the length of her spine. Thankfully she was immediately caught up in other introductions and relieved of the strain of Lord Hatherleigh's penetrating gaze. His eyes were blue, she noted, an unusual shade of grey blue. But that, of course, was to no point at all.

There were two other gentlemen to meet. Mr Cedric Cranfield was a tall, thin, fair-haired young man with prominent cheekbones and a removed, aloof attitude that did not encourage Kitty much in the task of conversing with him.

Sir William was completely different. Although he was middle-aged, his puce waistcoat, canary yellow pantaloons, and ridiculously high shirt points proclaimed him to be a dandy. But his manners were engaging and he talked with a great deal of animation.

Finally the group was admonished by their hostess to make themselves comfortable. Kitty found herself in a chair next to Lady Dinwiddie, seated across from Agatha, Lady Cranfield and Lord Hatherleigh, who together occupied a rather crowded settee. Teresa sat off a little to herself, nearer the door. Lord Dinwiddie, Mr. Cranfield and Sir William stood in a semicircle around the mantelpiece and formed a separate group and conversation.

Lemonade for the ladiés and ale for the gentlemen were accepted with alacrity, and Lady Cranfield seemed relieved to see an iced plum cake and a bowl of fruit being carried in by a footman. The gathering's fatigue and hunger thus sufficiently appeased, the conversation revived with added wit and energy.

"As you do not wish to be rude, dear aunt," said Agatha, "and will not ask Nathan how he received those dreadful scratches, I shall volunteer the information." She turned to the earl, tilted her head prettily and inquired, "You do not mind, my love?"

"Why should I mind?" her love replied disinterestedly.

Kitty shot a quick, questioning look at the earl. He must have been expecting some reaction from her, but he exasperated her by looking entirely unconcerned.

"It grew dark before my lord arrived at the Black Swan last evening," Agatha began, "and somewhere on the road he was very nearly run over by a coach . . . !"

"Two phaetons, Agatha," corrected Nathan, yawning slightly.

"Oh, yes! Two phaetons! But Nathan was ever so quick and managed to avoid what seemed to be certain death by deftly leading his horse to the side of the road with only seconds to spare! His horse panicked, however, and threw dear Nathan into a gorse bush!"

Here Kitty thought she surprised a look exchanged between Mr. Cranfield and Sir William. Lord Dinwiddie had stepped away to procure a third piece of plum cake, and the two gentlemen were silent at the moment and near enough to overhear the other conversation. Mr. Cranfield's brows had drawn together into a scowl, but Sir William seemed amused. They momentarily recomposed their expressions, however, and attended once again to their approaching host.

Though most of Agatha's narrative had been correct, perhaps the two gentlemen doubted its veracity. But why should they? Perhaps they were well enough acquainted with Lord Hatherleigh to conclude that the marks were a result of a less innocent encounter than one with a gorse bush! She glared at him suspiciously.

He had not tried to bed her, but what of other women? Perhaps women that used their nails freely at play instead of in defence of their virtue! The thought brought a blush to her cheeks, but, according to the stable boys' conversations, such things were not uncommon. Lord Hatherleigh, however, sat with an innocent air and received the two older women's congratulations on his clever and timely escape from danger with such serene forbearance that Kitty found herself excessively irritated with him.

She found she could not help herself. She determined to make it more difficult for him. So, with an air of bewilderment, she asked, "Such marks from a gorse bush, my lord? I should think the thick layer of leaves at this time of year would serve as some protection!"

"Under ordinary circumstances you are quite right, Miss Whitchurch," he drawled, looking at her through slightly lowered lids. "But this, unfortunately, was a diseased bush, half-dead, its branches quite bare of foliage . . . and positively treacherous.''

"How unlucky for you to have fallen atop such a one, when others, much softer, were undoubtedly all around,'' Kitty replied in the same guileless manner. She thought his mouth twitched, but she was not sure. He merely continued to look at her in the same polite, somewhat bored, manner.

"What a pretty pussy!'' cried Miss Bidwell, as Cleopatra sauntered across the carpet towards them. Kitty was not pleased at the diversion. Though she knew it was probably dangerous to indulge herself in baiting Lord Hatherleigh, she found she enjoyed it to a vast degree. The man was just too provoking.

"Will she come to me, Miss Whitchurch?'' asked Miss Bidwell as Cleopatra jumped onto Kitty's lap and began to work her paws and purr rhythmically in contentment.

"No, I'm afraid not. I have had her since a kitten and she is most devoted to me, she's almost eccentric if cats can be so,'' Kitty answered, recovering her peace of mind to a more comfortable degree by the simple act of stroking the satin-soft fur of her pet.

"I put up with the vexatious creature for Katherine's sake alone, I assure you,'' said Lady Dinwiddie to Lady Cranfield in a disdainful half whisper. "She is not satisfied to be indifferent, as most cats, but is absolutely unfriendly! I do not even dare to try to pet the thing!''

Since she had out-eaten even Lord Dinwiddie, Lady Cranfield had grown quite sleepy and could only manage a muffled, "La!"

"Godmama," cried Kitty playfully. "You know Cleopatra is harmless. She just does not wish to be handled. Please do not scold her within such easy earshot. I heard everything you said, and she, I'm sure, hears even better than I."

Lady Dinwiddie spluttered a half-hearted denial, but stopped short when Cleopatra turned a quelling, glistening, green-eyed stare directly at her.

"Years ago in the colonies, Miss Whitchurch," observed Lord Hatherleigh, "you might have been burned at the stake for a witch. Your hair—black as a raven's wing!—and your unusual green eyes are not dissimilar to your pet's. You look positively related." Kitty felt sure he wished to add, And your claws are equally as sharp, but in politeness he could not.

"Indeed," said Kitty, with raised brows and the coldest voice she could produce.

"You are so droll, Nathan," cried Agatha. "Isn't he droll, Aunt Louisa! Mama and I often say so...."

Lord Hatherleigh surprised everyone by standing up in the middle of Agatha's nonsensical speech to step purposely across the short distance to Kitty's chair. He stood looking down at her for a moment, then at her cat, then stooped and traced his forefinger around Cleopatra's ear. The cat ceased purring almost instantly, the paws stopped their ecstatic movements and Cleopatra looked up at him most forbiddingly.

"I pray you do not excite her, my lord," began Kitty, trying to speak calmly but really angry at Lord Hatherleigh for his audacity. The earl merely lifted a cautionary hand and bade her in a mild tone to please be silent. This was too much, and she was about to say so when Kitty noticed that Cleopatra's eyes were closing once again in drowsy response. Lord Hatherleigh dug his fingers gently into Cleopatra's fur, caressing the sensitive areas behind her ears and under her chin. Her purring resumed as before.

Kitty found the circumstance most vexing. Except for her father and her, no one had ever been able to bring about such a response in Cleopatra. But she would not reveal her astonishment to Lord Hatherleigh. She would not give him the pleasure.

"There, girl. You are really not so unapproachable, are you?" Nathan whispered caressingly and looked briefly up at Kitty to enjoy her discomfiture. He saw she was having a most difficult time masking her irritation, and he could not help but smile wickedly and add, "You are an intelligent creature, after all, Cleopatra. Wise enough, indeed, to recognize the touch of mastery and experience and enjoy the opportunity while you may." Without another look, he returned to his seat, leaving a pale Kitty quite beside herself with suppressed indignation and rage.

CHAPTER THREE

LATER THAT EVENING, as she dressed for dinner, Kitty found many different thoughts and feelings competing for her attention. Most persistently claiming her mind was the image of Lord Hatherleigh laughing up at her as he fondled her devoted pet. As she had done several times already that day, Kitty looked over at Cleopatra, who was reclining atop her armoire, and squinted her eyes into little slits of accusation. Cleopatra shifted uneasily and turned to watch the moving branches of a large elm tree just outside the window. A storm was brewing, both outside as well as in.

Another vexatious needle pricking Kitty was the fact that despite her previous experience with her persistent cousin, she had been miserably inept at warding off the earl's amorous advances. She had been taken by surprise, but she could not fully account for her lack of determined resistance while he had kissed her in that extremely...in that way. She touched her lips at the memory.

"Miss, you must stop fidgeting about if you expect your hair to be properly dressed for dinner," complained Leah. Lady Dinwiddie's abigail had taught

Leah how to arrange Kitty's hair in the current styles, but it was still a very serious and painstaking task for the older servant. Kitty determined to sit still.

And why should she be overset by the likes of such a man, anyway? she asked herself. She should be thinking about her future, which she did not intend to include a season in London. Her heart was irrevocably in the country, and she could not bear the thought of doing the pretty to a pack of primly proper dowagers at Almacks, or riding sedately through Hyde Park at the fashionable hour. She grimaced at the thought.

"Ain't I doing it right, miss?" was Leah's anxious reaction.

"Oh, yes! It's lovely, really, Leah," Kitty said, and smiled reassuringly. "Finish, please. I'm just restless." She decided she must learn to stop grimacing!

Matrimony. Now, that was her purpose. It *had* to be her purpose, for what other choice did she have? Her eyes misted suddenly as she thought of her father, but she forced back the mutinous tears and tried to think as dispassionately as possible about her situation.

Here, under Lady Dinwiddie's roof, were two very adequate prospects. Granted, both men had traits she could not admire, but she did not suppose that such a thing as a perfect man truly existed. And better still that they did not make her senses flutter, as she had once read in a romantical novel Lady Dinwiddie had lent her. This was to be a marriage of convenience.

She wished for nothing more than a comfortable home and the independence, as she saw it, of the wedded state.

Her mind wandered for a moment as she pondered the considerable disturbance her nerves underwent when she thought of Lord Hatherleigh's kiss—indeed when she thought of him at all! Could that singular sensation be considered a fluttering of her senses? She shook off the appalling thought forming in her head, however, and returned to the more important matters at hand.

Now which of the two should she set her cap for? Sir William had paid her a great deal of attention that afternoon, but Lady Dinwiddie proclaimed him to be a flirt. It was probably to be expected that he would single her out, as she was the only unspoken-for female there, besides Teresa Bidwell. And poor Miss Bidwell, with her unremarkable looks and diffident manner, was not the sort of girl men generally chose to flirt with. But Kitty knew that flirting frequently resulted in nothing more than a diverting memory to be indulged in on a dull day when one grew old. She wanted more than that!

Her only alternative, however, was Cedric Cranfield. But Kitty could not conceive how anyone could attract such a dull stick! It puzzled her why he had ever consented to be one of the party. He certainly was not enjoying himself. He had been Friday-faced and unapproachable the entire day and had not spoken much beyond the essential polite monosyllables. At least Sir William had spoken to her, and very flatteringly, too, she admitted.

Kitty was not so conceited as to believe that she might succeed easily with Sir William where others had failed, but she was also not so poor-spirited as to think it impossible! She would try her best, and with a little luck perhaps she would not have to endure a predatory season in town.

"How do I look, Leah?" asked Kitty at last, as she stood and made a graceful turn in front of her abigail. Kitty knew she was pretty, but the fact did not overly concern her or occupy her thoughts to any degree. For her present purposes, however, she knew it to be an asset.

"Like a bloomin' rose, miss," declared Leah with pride. A rose was an apt simile, for Kitty was dressed in a sleek silk gown of purest primrose, with a wreath of baby's breath to adorn her elegant coiffure. Her eyes sparkled and her lips and cheeks were fresh and pink. She descended the stairs quite determined to conquer.

Dinner did not encourage Kitty much, for though Lady Dinwiddie cleverly placed her between the two gentlemen whose fate she had been earlier planning, Sir William evidently left off flirting while sitting in front of a table laden with delicious food. He ate with relish and discussed each dish and its various healthful or unhealthful properties in detail and at great length. Mr. Cranfield simply ate, sparingly, and expressed no opinion whatsoever about his meal.

After dinner, when the ladies had left the men to their port and settled in the drawing room, Kitty found herself immediately accosted by Agatha.

"Kitty, you cannot imagine my delight when my aunt told me you were here!" she exclaimed, drawing her to a couch and fairly floating into place beside her. "I have never forgotten what fun we had together that lovely summer. I've wanted to visit my aunt on numerous occasions since then, but Mama has kept me excessively busy in town."

"Yes, I can readily believe that your social calendar is extremely hectic," said Kitty with an indulgent smile. Agatha had always been a little featherbrained, but her childlike ingenuousness was charming.

"Oh, yes! But Mama never seemed to tire and had no mercy on me! I went to more than one ball with an aching head and sore feet! But now that I am betrothed," she said with a soft little sigh, as she smoothed out the folds of her cornflower blue skirt, "I am allowed to relax. After all, Mama *has* gained her point."

"And to your taste, I conclude?" asked Kitty, her fine eyes opening wide in an expression of great interest.

"Oh, yes, of course! How could it be otherwise?" responded Agatha with what Kitty could only feel was an excess of enthusiasm. "Indeed, I cannot believe my great good luck!"

"Nonsense, Agatha," Kitty declared. "You are too modest."

"Oh, no, really I'm not being modest! You see, despite the long-held wishes of my dear mama that ours would be a match, I never expected it to occur. Lord Hatherleigh completely surprised me when he offered marriage. We have been attending the same parties, the same balls for the last two years. He was always polite when we met, but I don't think we ever had a conversation that lasted more than three minutes."

"But you must have seen a gradual change in his behaviour before he actually declared himself?"

"No, that is the most astonishing part of it all. Four weeks ago I was at a large party when he suddenly appeared and asked me to dance the quadrille. He was very talkative—that is, when the movements of the dance brought us together—and afterwards asked me to walk with him in the garden. I swear my heart pounded so I hardly knew what I said! But I must have said yes, because the next moment I found myself actually seated in an alcove, in a beautiful garden, with the elusive Lord Hatherleigh!" Here she paused and looked thoughtful, as if still trying to put the puzzle of that remarkable evening together.

"Agatha, you are not going to tell me that he declared himself to you that very night?" prompted an incredulous Kitty.

"I am indeed!" was her wondering reply. Then in a rather self-conscious voice, and looking down at her small hands twisting nervously in her lap, she said, "But I cannot answer yes to the next question I'm sure you're about to ask me."

"I'm afraid I don't know what you mean!"

"You aren't going to ask if he kissed me?" exclaimed Agatha with a look of disbelief.

"No! It would never occur to me to ask such an impertinent question!" It had never occurred to Kitty that he *wouldn't* have kissed her!

"You are odd! Everyone else asks me! And it's so distressing to have to tell them no! Sometimes I tell them it's none of their affair and they naturally assume that he did, and I do not have to lose face. In fact, though he was very polite," said Agatha, her winged brows drawing together slightly, "his whole manner of asking me was not nearly so charming as some of the other declarations I've received."

"But you said yes despite his mode of asking?"

"Of course! I told him I would not mind if he spoke to Mama. I would have been an absolute simpleton to say otherwise, Kitty!" She frowned briefly at her friend, as if astonished at her stupidity. "But, as I was saying," she continued, "it was so lucky that he should suddenly realize he wished to marry me, for Mama was in such a pucker over it. She had almost despaired of ever bringing Lord Hatherleigh up to scratch. I have had many requests for my hand, you know, but only the earl would satisfy her. Now that it is a fait accompli she is quite ecstatic!''

"Well, Agatha," said Kitty, secretly rather shocked at this glimpse into the matchmaking habits of the ton. "You have convinced me that your mother approves the match. Now, what about you? Do *you* like Lord Hatherleigh?"

"What a question, Kitty!" exclaimed Agatha, laughing affectedly. "Who could not?"

"Indeed," murmured Kitty. "Who could not?" But Agatha did not hear her because Lady Dinwiddie had produced a gaudy piece of needlepoint. She had been working on it as a covering for a cushion, and Agatha and her mother were in transports.

"It is divine!" declared Lady Cranfield, her several chins quivering in conjunction with the excited nodding of her head.

"Precious!" agreed Agatha, lifting her hands in delight.

"And what do you think, Miss Bidwell?" cried Lady Dinwiddie, pleased at the reception her craftsmanship had so far received. "I do not ask Katherine. She told me when she was a mere child what she thought of my needlework. Humph! But you are probably more used to doing this sort of thing than my goddaughter, and I trust you will be impartial, as my dear sister and Agatha can never be! I mean to give it to my older sister, Caroline, on her birthday. It is my own design! Do you think she will like it?"

The offensive article was thrust beneath Miss Bidwell's nose. Her dilemma was real. If she told Lady Dinwiddie the truth, that she found the conglomeration of cherubs, nymphs, flowers and birds overwhelming and not at all pleasing to the eye, she would be rude. She did not wish to offend such a kind and gracious hostess, or to comment on her florid, extravagant taste. And if Caroline were at all like her two sisters she would probably like the cushion very well.

"It is ... colourful. Yes, highly colourful!" pronounced Miss Bidwell at length, her relief at finding a safe adjective quite evident to Kitty. "Your sister, if she is at all like you, Lady Dinwiddie, will like it excessively."

Lady Dinwiddie was satisfied by the ambiguous praise, and Kitty, impressed by Teresa's handling of the situation, drew near. The two others still hovered over Lady Dinwiddie and were suggesting the addition of a unicorn.

"You are from Hertfordshire, Miss Bidwell?" asked Kitty with an encouraging smile. Miss Bidwell responded immediately to Kitty's warmth.

"Yes!" She paused wistfully. "It's lovely there! But perhaps everyone speaks of their home in such terms," she added apologetically.

"Perhaps. But only if they were happy there," replied Kitty, suspecting that Miss Bidwell had been extremely happy. "Are you a large family?"

"I've seven younger brothers," confided Miss Bidwell, "and so many cats and dogs I've claimed for my own over the years, they, too, must be considered part of my family!" She chuckled pleasantly, then sighed. "I miss them all, of course. But I certainly would not have been welcome to join Agatha for a season in town had I brought along even one of my pets. Like your godmother, Lady Cranfield does not like cats or dogs. She says they are as much trouble and responsibility as children. But then she has not encountered my riotous little brothers! They are a handful, even for Papa!"

Kitty laughed with her, imagining just the sort of normal boys the Bidwell brothers undoubtedly were. Sitting thus with Miss Bidwell, Kitty contemplated the perverse nature of man. This young woman had a delightful quickness of mind and a sweetness of disposition that any right-minded gentleman ought to treasure in a life's companion, but no gentleman had evidently been able to get past her plain face to appreciate her inner beauty. Lady Dinwiddie had told her that Teresa Bidwell was twenty-three years old, well on her way to spinsterhood. What a pity! Miss Bidwell would be an excellent wife and mother if given the opportunity.

The men did not linger long over their drinks, and it was, in fact, Sir William who led them into the drawing room with an eager step. Kitty looked up and smiled with suitable shyness when her intended target seemed to hesitate in the middle of the room.

Her aim hit the mark and he seated himself beside her. Just then there was a resounding clap of thunder.

"La!" exclaimed Lady Dinwiddie amidst other expressions of surprise and dismay. "We talked of having an excursion to the abbey ruins on the morrow, but it does not look as if we shall!"

Kitty grimaced and glanced towards the window.

"You do not like such storms, Miss Whitchurch?" suggested Sir William, taken aback by the unladylike expression on her face.

Kitty mentally kicked herself and forced her recalcitrant lips into a sweet, beguiling smile. "They are well enough in the winter, Sir William, but I cannot like them in the summer when I long to be outside. I am disappointed that our excursion is to be put off."

"Do not despair, Miss Whitchurch" was Sir William's bracing reply. "We shall have our excursion as soon as possible, when I shall take great pleasure in seeing you amongst the summer blooms! You shall put them positively to shame!"

Kitty thought to herself that it was he who would be most likely to upstage the flowers, with his tangerine waistcoat, his lace-edged, brilliantly white cravat tied in the intricate Mathematical, and the numerous fobs, chains and rings that shone on various parts of his person. But she only fluttered her lashes and looked demurely at the tips of her satin slippers.

"In the meantime," he continued, "we must employ ourselves with conversation, music, whist and piquet. It is no hardship for me, I assure you. We are, after all, a delightful group. A group, in short, with whom I should not mind finding myself marooned, if needs be, for the duration of a blizzard!"

"Your indefatigable spirits put me quite to the blush, sir," simpered Kitty. "I am cheered despite myself!"

"Such is my aim, Miss Whitchurch" was his gallant reply. "For to tell truth, it is your society that makes my stay here at Ridley so truly amiable!"

Kitty acknowledged this latest compliment with a flirtatious wave of her fan and turned away, only to encounter a look of barely contained amusement on the face of Lord Hatherleigh. She had been assiduously avoiding that gentleman and was not pleased to find him leaning against the mantelpiece and so close as to have overheard her entire conversation with Sir William.

She was momentarily discomposed, but fortified herself with the thought that she did not care a fig for such a man's opinion. Agatha's disclosure of his hasty manner of procuring her hand in marriage was just further proof of his great conceit. He had obviously had no fear of Agatha's refusing him. Such arrogance did not bear thinking of, she concluded, throwing him a look of utter contempt. She then turned back to Sir William with a smile and resumed her strategy as before.

"And how long, sir, do you plan to delight us with your company?"

What followed was a monologue from Sir William about how unhealthful lengthy stays in town could be and how he should be perfectly happy to remain in the country indefinitely if only his tailor were not so indispensable to him. He found it necessary to visit that establishment at least twice a month.

MUCH LATER, after Kitty had excused herself on the pretext of having the headache, she slipped outside by the servants' entrance to the back of the kitchen. She breathed in the damp, invigorating air washed clean by the rain.

She looked up at a sky that was still unsettled. The moon was full and clouds streamed swiftly across it; at one moment its light shone brightly on the kitchen garden, glistening on the dark leaves, and the next moment it vanished, leaving only shadows of varying shapes and sizes.

Kitty made her way carefully along the stone walk that wound through the garden. At the end was a gate that led into the formal grounds. Here were flower beds laid out in an orderly fashion, much too precise to suit Kitty.

She hurried now, as the walk was broader and the moonlight unobscured for the moment. Her object was to find her way to the estate's small lake located just far enough beyond the carefully clipped lawns and pruned shrubs to have been allowed to remain in its natural state.

When she finally came upon the lake she could not help a small exclamation of delight. It seemed almost enchanted. Small ripples in the water reflected the scattered patches of light, while shadows drifted across its surface. The wind was stronger now and the trees swayed before its force. The sound of the high, rustling leaves charged the air with an earthy energy Kitty could feel quivering at the very centre of her being.

Turning into the wind, she walked in long, slow steps along the shore. Her hair blew loose from its pins and the tangled tresses streamed behind her and across her face. But Kitty didn't care—indeed she did not even notice. She was lost in a deep sense of kinship with this night and its restless movements. At the hall she must act the schoolroom miss, sweet and biddable, but here she could be free and as natural as her surroundings.

She walked in this way for several minutes until it began to rain again. She looked around for shelter, then remembered a structure she had passed on her way around the lake. Years ago, Lord Dinwiddie had constructed a landing dock that was about twice the usual width. He had instructed the carpenter to build a closely latticed framework over the top and along the sides sufficient to support the growth of vines. This was done, the seeds were planted, and over the years the thick vines had created an arch of greenery to shelter occasional walkers from the sun. Tonight Kitty hoped it would prove equally valuable as refuge from a storm. Beginning to feel the cool rain penetrate her thin gown, she turned back and ran towards it.

She stopped, startled, just inside the deck. With the sudden onset of rain her sanctuary was like a dark and not particularly inviting tunnel. Where a dim light shone in the farther opening she saw a rowboat tied to the dock. She could hear the soft lapping of water and watched as the boat rose and fell with the swelling motion of the agitated lake.

Then at the edge of the dock itself, she noticed something else. A champagne bottle and a crystal glass? Was she seeing things? But there they were, their unmistakable shapes silhouetted against the watery grey background. She pondered several explanations when a hand suddenly appeared out of the shadows and picked up the glass. A tall form advanced in her direction. Her body jerked back involuntarily at the unexpected presence. Her mouth opened, but without producing a sound. Her feet seemed to be fastened to the dock.

"Miss Whitchurch, pray do not be alarmed," said the cool voice of Lord Hatherleigh. "It is only I."

"You! What are you doing out here?"

"I might ask you the same question," he replied quizzingly. "Most ladies of my acquaintance find lavender water on a lace handkerchief pressed against their brow much more conducive to treating the headache than wandering around in the rain.'' He demonstrated the feminine attitude for her, but it was still too dark for Kitty to see, and his mime went unappreciated. ''I must say, though, Miss Whitchurch, that you disappoint me. Could you not come up with something better than the headache? I had thought you would be more original!''

''I did have the headache, my lord,'' she declared with asperity, ''but the state of my health can be no concern of yours!''

''Come over here by the light—what there is of it—so that I may see your face as we talk,'' he suggested, ignoring her remark. He put his hand on her elbow and drew her to the end of the dock, and she allowed it because she was decidedly ill at ease standing thus in the shadows.

''I did not think you would go directly to bed when you left us, Miss Whitchurch,'' he continued, when they emerged into the thin moonlight that managed to escape between the scuttling clouds. ''The look on your face just before you left the room reminded me of a certain caged orangutan I saw at the menagerie in London last year....''

''I beg your pardon!'' she exclaimed with unfeigned shock and revulsion. ''You odious creature! How dare you compare me to such a wild hairy, vulgar creature!''

''Oh, do forgive me,'' he hastily interjected, choking back a chuckle. ''Indeed, I do not mean to say you resemble an orangutan in any way. I find you decidedly attractive, as you must know! But the poor animal I speak of looked frantic to flee. So did you, Miss Whitchurch. That is all I meant.''

When he received no response to this beyond stony, unrelenting silence, he sighed and with a self-deprecatory chuckle, said, ''I seem to say and do everything which is most irritating to you, Miss Whitchurch. I . . .''

''And don't tell me you don't do it on purpose!'' she snapped, instantly ashamed at the peevish tone of her voice.

''I will admit to some enjoyment at your expense,'' the earl ruefully acknowledged, ''but you must believe me,'' he went on in a more sober tone, ''this morning I honestly thought you to be in the employ of that avaricious innkeeper. Not satisfied with plumping his pockets at my expense, he fairly drove me from a pleasant game of cards with his constant badgering. He could not accept that I had no desire to indulge myself with one of his choice bits of finery.'' He paused. ''I sincerely apologize for my, er, actions this morning.''

Much against Kitty's inclination, she was placated by the earl's apology. He sounded quite sincere, and he deserved at least some recognition for it, she supposed.

''Well, I may forgive you, but only if you will stop annoying me,'' she suggested hopefully.

"Miss Whitchurch," he responded with a devilish grin, "I should choose then to be unforgiven, for I do so enjoy annoying you."

"Stop talking such drivel," she declared, stamping her foot against the dock's floor, causing the structure to sway slightly.

"Then let us continue our previous conversation. I assert that you wished to leave your company this evening as much as the aforementioned orangutan wished to leave his cage."

"You are wrong," she stated flatly, folding her arms in a stubborn gesture across her chest. "I found the company this evening—most of it, anyway—delightful!"

"Give over, my girl!" gently derided the earl. "No one with any sense could stand to listen to that rattle Stonebridge for any length of time!"

"You're wrong, I tell you," she reiterated.

"Well, as you say, then," he conceded, throwing up his hands in mock surrender. "Far be it from me to contradict a lady."

Silence reigned for a minute or two and Kitty began to wonder if she'd imagined his apology, when Lord Hatherleigh abruptly spoke again. "Though it is singular for a girl of your tender age, you aren't the least romantical, are you, Miss Whitchurch?"

Taken aback by the forthrightness of his remark, she proudly flung back, "Not in the least!"

"I suspected as much." He paused consideringly. "And you no doubt deplore the silly, simpering ways adopted by other young females?"

"Quite so!" Then, remembering Agatha, she added, "There are sensible young women, of course. It is the others I deplore. But I cannot blame them entirely for their goosishness. I daresay they cannot help it. Their mothers set the example for them and their fathers expect it of them."

"Yes, that's true. But you have not had any such influence exerted over you. Therefore I must conclude that the reason you have been employing the wiles you so despise is to fix Sir William's interest. A most unromantic figure, Will Stonebridge, but well enough for someone, like yourself, who does not require romance—only a few thousand a year."

Kitty gasped. "How dare you speak so to me—"

"Oh, do not look that way, and do not deny it! I saw what you were about in there, and I tell you that it is not possible. Pray listen to me, for I mean this kindly! I wish only to spare you a deal of trouble, for you cannot claim the fellow! I need not scruple to spare your more tender feelings, Miss Whitchurch, as I am convinced there are none involved. You are not romantical and have set your cap for Stonebridge for reasons solely practical. Save your efforts, my dear, and keep them for a more likely candidate. Sir William cannot be brought up to scratch, even by such a clever, fetching girl as you!"

Too incensed by this patronizing speech to consider even feigning a disinterest in Sir William, Kitty heatedly declared, "Well, we shall see about that, won't we? You are so puffed up by your own imagined consequence that you think you can dictate the lives of everyone about you!"

"No, you mistake my motives," he assured her with an air of much-tried patience. "It is simply that I know the fellow well, and could tell you tales about him that would amply discourage your determined pursuit. He has eluded sophisticated town beauties, with all their matchmaking mamas for the past fifteen years. No easy task, that! He will not succumb to your charms, Miss Whitchurch, considerable though they are! Certainly not to the point of matrimony. Though you have espoused the cynical philosophy of our society, and are bent on a marriage of convenience, you are, after all, a mere country chit, and a hoyden at that! Your act is well done, but in view of the odds against you, I advise—"

"I need no advice from you!" she ground out between clenched teeth with such ferocity that Lord Hatherleigh's brows rose quite out of sight into the fringe of his black hair.

"You are determined to waste your time, then?"

"I don't think I shall be wasting my time," fumed Kitty, finding her usual self-control somehow evaporating when she had to deal with the earl. Thrusting her chin forward, she blurted out, "Why...why,

I'll just wager he will not find me so unsuitable a wife as..."

"Just what will you wager?" Lord Hatherleigh interjected softly. "What have you worth wagering in all the world, Miss Whitchurch?"

"I did not mean to say..." she spluttered confusedly.

"You have proposed a wager," he persisted, with an odd, twisted smile on his lips. "And I am happy to accept. You see I am persuaded you will lose, and I cannot resist a sure thing." He continued to stare at her with that strange smile transforming his face into something half-fiendish, half-tender in the freakish, erratic shadows of the wind-tossed vines. Kitty felt a convulsive shudder snake down her spine under the spell of that look. He turned abruptly away and reached into his waistcoat pocket to remove an elegant gold snuffbox and to take a pinch.

Kitty somehow found her voice. "How can you be so sure!" she burst out, feeling as if she would explode at any moment. She had had no intention of placing a wager on her ability to ensnare Sir William, since she had never, even at her most sanguine, felt absolutely sure of the outcome. Why, she had only met the man that day and only hours before had she decided to try to win him. But Lord Hatherleigh's complete lack of belief in her abilities was utterly exasperating! Oh, how she wished to show him otherwise!

She struggled with herself for several minutes, but common sense finally prevailed and she began to retreat. "I have no respectable amount of money to place on a wager, Lord Hatherleigh," she said in tones of reason, "and as I did not really intend to..."

"I'll take your Jezebel. She's a fine piece of horseflesh, that one."

"But I do not wish to wager at all!" she cried in frustration.

"Didn't your father teach you, Miss Whitchurch, to honour your word?" he coolly inquired. When she had no ready retort, but instead grew absolutely rigid, he pressed his advantage with an exaggerated sigh, saying, "Well, if you are so sure you cannot bring the fellow up to scratch, I suppose I must release you from this most imprudent wager."

He turned to face the water and stood sipping his champagne. The only sound was the patter of rain, the water lapping against the dock and an occasional distant roll of thunder.

Kitty was trying to control the raging tumult of her feelings. She did not want to lose her horse, but she would vastly enjoy showing the earl that she was not just a silly, hoydenish girl from the country, unable to attract a city beau! She knew if she agreed to a wager with Lord Hatherleigh she would do anything, absolutely *anything* to achieve Sir William and thus assure Jezebel's safe-keeping.

She turned, as her companion had, to face the lake and though the multitude of little circles created in the water by the raindrops might have delighted her under ordinary circumstances, she was now too deep in thought to pay them any heed.

Was it possible she had met Lord Hatherleigh only that morning? How could one man have such a capacity for confusing, frustrating and, above all, irritating her in so short a time? As if in answer, all the events of the day passed through her mind, from his humiliating assumption this morning when he had kissed her to his unwelcome handling of Cleopatra to Agatha's revelation concerning their hasty engagement, and lastly to his scornful view of her abilities in regard to Sir William.

Well, she concluded to herself with a determined grimace, so shall it be! In as short a time as she could possibly manage, she *would* be Sir William's blushing bride! She could not wait until the moment she could throw her wedding ring directly into Lord Hatherleigh's face!

Having made a decision, Kitty hoped her voice, at least, was in reasonable control. She quietly asked, "And what will you wager, my lord?"

The rain subsided and the clouds were thinning out. Once more they moved in long streaks across the moon, casting eerie blue-white patches of illumination on Lord Hatherleigh's face. He did not answer immediately, as if he were thinking it over, and she continued to watch the play of light on his strong, aristocratic features.

He seemed to sense her scrutiny and turning with an amused smile, "I'd offer myself..."

"Do not be absurd!" she sniffed derisively, but her heart skipped a beat and resumed its steady rhythm only after a loud thump Kitty felt to the tips of her toes.

"Then it will have to be one hundred pounds." He smiled provocatively. "Do we have an agreement?"

"Yes, my lord, we do!" she staunchly agreed, wrenching her gaze away from the glittering seduction of his eyes. "Now, as it no longer rains, I shall be leaving."

"But it does still rain, Miss Whitchurch." He lazily reached his upturned palm out over the lake.

"Mere drizzle," she scornfully replied, with a dismissive wave of her hand. "And even if it were a deluge, and I were to get wet through and die of an inflammation of the lung as a result, I should still prefer it to staying here with you!"

Lord Hatherleigh had just brought his glass of champagne to his lips but choked on the contents. He was diverted beyond endurance by this last speech and could not help but laugh loudly and wholeheartedly.

Kitty was torn between the urge to laugh with him—oh, how her body and mind needed the release of a good laugh!—and the desire to push him into the lake. Her pride and her conscience, however, spoke in unison and she knew that neither action would be appropriate. Deciding instead to flee temptation, she turned and left the dock immediately, but the deep, melodious sounds of his mirth relentlessly followed her as she made her way back across the wet expanse of garden to Ridley Hall.

CHAPTER FOUR

"I HOPE YOU DO NOT MIND putting off our picnic for another day, Katherine," said Lady Dinwiddie, as she pulled on a pair of lavender gloves. They matched her Venetian lace shawl and her hat, an elaborate confection of purple ostrich feathers trembling precariously atop her head. "But the ground is still damp and I do not like the look of those clouds to the south. In any event, I have promised to take my sister to call on several of our near neighbours. She has not seen them for an age!"

"It doesn't matter, Godmama," responded Kitty, eyeing the purple bonnet with misgiving, fully expecting it to topple at any moment. She sat in that lady's boudoir where she had been summoned directly after breakfast. Lady Dinwiddie wished to discuss what the young people planned to do now that they had been denied their expedition.

"Agatha wishes to visit the Trumpington milliners," Kitty told her, "and the gentlemen do not object to escorting us on such feminine errands."

"Ah! That is very well, because I wish you to look at a length of silk for yourself, Katherine," said Lady

Dinwiddie, tugging on the ends of the huge purple bow tied beneath her plump chin.

"Whatever for? I have gowns enough now to last me a lifetime!"

"But not a ball gown, child."

"Is there to be a ball in the neighbourhood? I don't recall your mentioning one, Godmama."

"Oh, didn't I?" chuckled Lady Dinwiddie. "My lamentable memory! But after all, it was only last night that my lord and I decided to give you one! Mrs. Wells will protest that there is not time enough to open up the Crystal Room and have it up to snuff by next Tuesday, but she may get as many girls from the village as she wishes to help! And so I shall also give leave to Cook to get extra help in the kitchen, for my heart is quite set on it."

"You don't mean to say you're having a ball for me!" exclaimed Kitty. She was rather surprised but not displeased. She had been taught to dance but had never been to a ball or even an assembly in Trumpington! As a member of the old and respected Whitchurch family she had been punctiliously invited to all the gatherings sponsored by the local gentry, but she had refused every one. She had a notion that dancing with other young people might be very pleasurable, for she had even felt considerable enjoyment in the company of her stiff dancing instructor. But her dislike of leaving her father alone and the expense of actually having to buy an appropriate dress inevitably kept her away.

"Kitty, you do not dislike the idea, do you?" Lady Dinwiddie anxiously enquired. Kitty had been remarkably cooperative so far, and her godmother lived in constant dread lest she regress to her former ways.

"Dislike it? No, indeed! I like it excessively!"

Much comforted by this information, Lady Dinwiddie nodded her approval and manoeuvred her stiff skirts through the door and down to the drawing room with a light heart.

Kitty followed closely behind, tying her Chippendale bonnet embellished with a single daisy as she went. The simple hat perfectly complemented the soft yellow frock she wore. But Kitty was not thinking about her looks.

She was determining just how to ensure Sir William as her supper companion at the ball. She had to admit that though she had entered unwillingly into her wager with Lord Hatherleigh, it lent an additional challenge to her pursuit of Sir William. Her real regret was that the whole deplorable agreement had all come about through her own sad lack of control. She had always been proud of her cool head and presence of mind. But thus far every encounter she had had with the earl had ended in her decided discomfiture.

Entering the drawing room, Kitty quickly observed that everyone was present except Sir William and Agatha. No one asked where they were, because everyone, including Kitty, had come to realize that being late was habitual for them.

"Well, sister, we are off!" cried Lady Dinwiddie as Hiller announced the readiness of their carriage. "My lord has taught me never to keep the horses waiting, haven't you, dearest? Goodbye, my love! Goodbye to you all! We shall see you at dinner!"

Both women then made their exit in a flurry of rustling skirts, leaving behind the pungent combination of fragrances they had both so liberally applied to their persons. Hiller, who had been holding the door, coughed discreetly and walked away, seeking fresh air. Lord Dinwiddie left soon after, equally overcome.

The remaining occupants were a group very unlikely to provide entertainment for a lively young woman. Miss Bidwell had unluckily been forced to find a seat near Mr. Cranfield and was too shy to strike up a conversation. He looked as stiff and priggish as usual and maintained an unbroken silence.

Kitty seated herself in the chair nearest the door and carefully avoided looking at Lord Hatherleigh. He stood by the mantel and she could feel him looking at her. Presently he detached himself to approach her. She had picked up some needlework and for appearance's sake was halfheartedly jabbing at it. He leaned over as if to admire it.

Kitty was well aware that it was ill done and was compelled by honesty to say, "It's not very good. Not a talent of mine, I'm afraid."

"Quite so," he murmured, lifting the quizzing glass that hung from a ribbon about his neck and peering through it in a finicky way.

She had a strong desire to stab him with her needle.

"Don't think of it, I pray," he admonished, glancing up from the embroidery hoop.

His amusement was evident, and Kitty savagely replaced her needle in the pincushion before icily enquiring, "How may I help you, my lord?"

"Is it not strange, Miss Whitchurch, that you and I—and even Lady Dinwiddie—are perfectly able to ready ourselves for a trip to town—a small market town at that—within the space of an hour, but our missing companions utterly lack this ability? I did not hurry, I assure you. Nor, I imagine, did you. But here we are, and they are undoubtedly still at their toilettes."

"I do not doubt it, my lord," replied Kitty primly. "But what does it signify?"

"Only that I shall probably find myself standing, or most probably sitting, just so innumerable times once I am married to Agatha. And so, too, will you find yourself, Miss Whitchurch, if you should marry Sir Will. But I am a patient man. A young woman with your volatile disposition, however..." He paused dramatically. "I hope you have considered every disadvantage of such a connection."

Kitty turned to give her determined antagonist a sharp look and an equally sharp retort, only to be momentarily put off by the expression of unholy glee she encountered as their eyes met. Oh, how he did enjoy baiting her! Despite this observation, or perhaps because of it—Kitty wasn't sure which—she opened her mouth to speak, but the stinging words were not to be said.

The two subjects of their conversation immediately appeared and the entire party was soon comfortably settled within Lord Dinwiddie's dove-grey-and-pearl travelling chaise and the horses urged to a lively trot. Looking at Sir William and Agatha, each extravagantly and flawlessly dressed, Kitty resentfully decided that if they had to be tardy they could have at least timed it so that she might have spoken her mind to Lord Hatherleigh.

It was a beautiful summer day, despite the slight scattering of fluffy white clouds that Lady Dinwiddie had found so threatening. Kitty wished she might forget the others and lose herself in the verdant landscape around her. But, alas, she knew she would not win Sir William by sitting passively. She applied herself to her task immediately by exclaiming upon the brilliant cut of his coat.

It was an extremely productive opening, as it kept Sir William agreeably occupied in detailing the numerous styles of neck cloths that particularly complemented that type of cut. This recital lasted right up to the moment they turned onto the main thoroughfare of Trumpington.

Agatha began to chatter excitedly about the additional shops that had opened since she last had visited the town. In one window an especially fetching bonnet caught her eye and she beseeched the driver to pull over at once. He did as she bade and they were soon inside the shop examining its various confections.

Agatha was ecstatic over the bonnet, which, to her utter delight, had a matching parasol. In a remote, patronizing tone of voice, Lord Hatherleigh offered to buy the fripperies for her as part of her many engagement presents, and Agatha squealed in delight.

If not for the matter of age, thought Kitty, they could have been mistaken for an indulgent father or great-uncle bestowing a gift on a spoilt but endearing child.

"Oh! Miss Whitchurch?"

Kitty turned at the soft, childish voice and saw, standing irresolutely at the door of the establishment, a tiny, large-eyed girl she knew very well.

"Susan!" exclaimed Kitty, walking quickly over to the thin, shabbily dressed child. "What are you doing in town all by yourself?"

"Mum sent me for a bit o' bread, miss. Little Johnny has wailed this whole day, and poor Mum didn't dare to put 'im down to bake bread, not even a biscuit!"

"The baby is ill?" Kitty questioned, concern wrinkling her smooth brow.

"Yes'm. And Mum can't tell what the matter is." She gazed up imploringly at Kitty. "It has been so long since you've come to see us. Not since yer pa..."

"I know, Susan," said Kitty, suddenly very conscience-stricken. "I've been terribly busy. It was remiss of me, though. Will you forgive me if I come with you now?"

"Oh, miss! Would you?" Her little face lit up at the prospect.

"Oh course! And we'll buy something to go with the bread you have fetched like a good girl for your mother." She smiled reassuringly, then suddenly remembered her other companions and turned back to face them.

Sir William stood at some distance eyeing the child rather dubiously. Agatha was clutching her reticule as if the poor little thing might make off with it at any moment. Miss Bidwell looked pityingly at the child, and Mr. Cranfield appeared as serious as always. As for Lord Hatherleigh, he leaned against a table covered with ribbons and lace and gazed intently from her to Susan and back again. What he might have been thinking she could not guess.

"This is Susan," Kitty said. "She is the daughter of a woman who worked for us at Whitchurch until Susan here came into the world, about six years ago." She smiled kindly down at the child again.

Susan had grown progressively less shy and was now leaning fondly against Kitty, hanging on to her skirts.

"I used to visit them at least every other week, but I'm afraid I have grown neglectful of late. Do you mind terribly if I leave you to help Susan procure some provisions for the family and to look in at the baby? They live on the outskirts of town and I promise not to tarry."

No one responded. Indeed, thought Kitty, they all looked to be tongue-tied.

"Well? Gentlemen, Agatha, Miss Bidwell, what do you say?" prompted Kitty.

"Of... of course, Kitty, if you wish," stammered Agatha, still looking anxiously at the child. "We can take tea and a cold collation at the inn and wait for you there."

"I think not," interjected Lord Hatherleigh curtly, and Agatha was immediately silenced. "Miss Whitchurch has no maid with her. We shall accompany her on whatever errands she deems necessary to be of service to her friends."

Surprised and irritated by Lord Hatherleigh's dictatorial manner of speaking to his fiancée, Kitty was about to refuse his offer when Mr. Cranfield stepped away from Miss Bidwell and drew near to Agatha.

He rested his thin white hand on her shoulder and, looking at Kitty rather than his stepsister, said, "We cannot let you go unattended, Miss Whitchurch. She looks to be a good little girl, and if the truth be known, it cannot hurt us to forgo our selfish pursuits this once for an obvious case of charity. I know we must all feel equally upon the subject.''

Agatha instantly blushed a most becoming shade of pink and smiled understandingly at Mr. Cranfield. Kitty's mouth almost fell open at this revelation of Mr. Cranfield's character. She had never dreamed he harboured such feelings. Lord Hatherleigh, however, observed this affecting scene impassively and, discovering a bit of lint on his coat sleeve, flicked it away.

''Indeed we do,'' agreed Miss Bidwell warmly. ''Where shall we go first, Miss Whitchurch?'' she asked, overcoming her diffidence and eager to take part in this errand of mercy.

''Yes, where?'' said Agatha, emboldened by Mr. Cranfield's support.

Belatedly realizing that he must appear meanspirited before the benevolent and lovely Miss Whitchurch if he did not join in the general enthusiasm, Sir William said with a gallant air that he should be most happy to help Miss Whitchurch with her packages.

Kitty saw that they could not be dissuaded, but she determined that their elegant presence would not hinder her efforts. So she led them from one shop to another gathering those necessities she deemed most useful for the immediate relief of the impoverished family.

Kitty's entourage attracted much interest from passers-by. It was certainly uncommon to see such a group of swells undertaking the mundane shopping and carrying that would ordinarily be done by their servants. But if the onlookers were amazed by the spectacle they presented, none could be more amazed than Sir William and Agatha.

It seemed that neither of them had ever been inside the door of a butcher shop, and they looked on with a mixture of disgust and admiration as Kitty picked out a pair of stewing chickens and a joint of mutton with apparent knowledge and discrimination. Kitty did not dare to look at Lord Hatherleigh, but talked almost exclusively to Susan until they had finished their shopping and found themselves at last at the door of her parents' humble cottage.

"Mum, look!" cried Susan, as she drew Kitty into the small parlour, holding fast to her hand.

There was a slight youngish woman sitting by the hearth in a reed-backed rocker. She held a stout baby, who, for the moment, had fallen into a feverish sleep. As Kitty hastened over, she saw that his face was flushed and his lips dry.

"Miss, I'm right glad at the sight of you, I kin tell you!" Mrs. Kimball exclaimed, a look of relief lighting her tired, worried face. "Poor Johnny is so—"

She stopped suddenly as she caught sight of the other faces staring in at the door. Kitty saw her bewilderment and hurriedly explained as she motioned the others to come in.

"These are friends of mine, Emily. Lord Hatherleigh, Lady Agatha Middlemiss, Sir William Stonebridge, Mr. Cranfield and Miss Bidwell. They were in town with me and kindly offered to escort." She turned to the others, "This is Mrs. Kimball."

They all nodded rather uncomfortably in acknowledgement of the introductions, and Kitty realized that a bow or a handshake would have been quite impossible for all three gentlemen still held armfuls of bulky packages.

"Oh, please put those on the table just inside the kitchen there," said Kitty, pointing at the only other door.

"I'll show you!" cried Susan, proud to be of help as she led the gentlemen away.

"I've brought everything you'll need for a hearty, nourishing soup, Emily," Kitty went on. "And bread and butter and some beautiful pippins. The joint of mutton will do for tomorrow. I hope Johnny is well enough then that you may cook your dinner unimpeded by the poor dear's cries. Is he terribly warm? He looks it." She stooped to look closer at the baby, but did not wish to touch him for fear of waking him up.

"He's been feverish this whole day, but naught else seems to be amiss. He sucks a little and keeps it down. It's just he's been so terrible hot," responded Mrs. Kimball.

"Sleep will do him good and you need the rest, too, so I'll just start the soup," Kitty said, straightening and beginning to pull off her white kid gloves.

"No, you mustn't!" cried Mrs. Kimball, immediately waking Johnny, who whimpered pitiably and moved restlessly in his mother's arms. "I can't have a lady such as you, miss, in my kitchen mucking about in that pretty dress. Johnny is woken now. Here, do hold him, miss, whilst I start the soup."

Kitty was not averse to this suggestion, and just as she took the fussy child in her arms, the gentlemen returned to the parlour. Mrs. Kimball went straightaway into the kitchen. Kitty knew she must have been very eager to rid herself of such intimidating company and sympathized with her wholeheartedly. She wished she had not had to bring the lot of them along.

Johnny did not howl, but he moaned and whimpered and tossed his chubby arms and legs back and forth in protest. Kitty cooed and bounced him as she walked about the room.

Miss Bidwell watched for as long as she could constrain herself, then walked up to Kitty and, holding out her arms, said, "Oh, please, Miss Whitchurch, let me! He reminds me of my smallest brother, Andrew. And I'm said to have a way with the little ones!"

"I'm sure you do," said Kitty, smiling warmly at Miss Bidwell as she relinquished the agitated bundle to her more experienced arms. But she watched, fascinated, as her shy friend diverted Johnny from his misery with a sweet, soothing melody, and a gentle swaying. Kitty thought of her cousin Sarah and wondered how that new little babe and his mother fared.

All this time Agatha had hovered just inside the front door. Her eyes were wide and unsure in her small, pale face, and she had not uttered a word. She had never been in such close proximity to poverty. Her mother was not the charitable sort, and thus Agatha had never been expected to visit or assist the less fortunate, or to take part in any of the activities that were so familiar to Kitty.

Indeed, Agatha seemed to shrink further and further into the woodwork, and Kitty wondered why Lord Hatherleigh did not go to his fiancée instead of staring so fixedly at Johnny and Miss Bidwell. However, Mr. Cranfield came to his stepsister's rescue once more. It was subtly done. He only drew near enough so that Agatha might grasp his arm, and though he said nothing, he had evidently imparted some of his own unshakable calm to her.

Sir William was equally uncomfortable, but he wished to impress Kitty. He drew close to her and, gazing down at the child in Miss Bidwell's arms, asked with unconvincing interest, "What is the little fellow's age, Miss Whitchurch? He seems a strapping sort!"

"He is but five months old, but is big like his father. I hope he is not very ill."

"Ill? The child is ill?" Sir William exclaimed, stepping hurriedly back. "You did not tell me there would be sick children here! You do not think he is infectious, do you? I am never around infants, you know. Meg couldn't give me any, more's the pity, and now I recall hearing that the little things are prone to all manner of unfortunate illnesses! Oh, I do believe I have been much remiss in entering this abode at all, Miss Whitchurch!" His eyes darted around the small room as if contagion lurked in its very walls. He took out a pale yellow mono-grammed handkerchief and began mopping his brow, which had suddenly grown damp.

At first Kitty could only gaze at Sir William in speechless wonder. She knew he was a dandy, but surely not such an old fusspot as to be put off by a childish fever! After all, every trifling thing raised a child's temperature, didn't it? And she had told them, hadn't she, that the baby was ill? She cast her mind back to their first encounter with Susan at the millinery shop. Well, perhaps she hadn't precisely said the child was ill, and, come to think of it, they probably hadn't heard anything of her initial con-versation with Susan. Oh, dear, perhaps they wouldn't have come with her at all if they'd known!

Grasping the enormity of her error at having ex-posed her fainthearted matrimonial target to a pos-sible head cold, Kitty struggled for something to say that might soothe Sir William's ruffled composure. But what?

"I think I must really wait in the carriage, Miss Whitchurch," that gentleman finally muttered, while she still sought the proper phrase to reassure her anxious suitor. "My health is precarious y'know, very precarious. Can't take chances, you understand."

He headed for the door and was almost run over by two other small children just returning to the house with baskets of berries on their arms. He stiffened, then sidled past them and strode hastily to the carriage.

Kitty looked after him in chagrin. She was, however, unexpectedly saved from falling into self-reproach by Lord Hatherleigh. His lordship startled everyone in the room by taking a sudden choking spell. The paroxysm was so intense that he was compelled to remove his handkerchief and cover his entire face with it, retiring to a corner until the attack abated.

Miss Bidwell clucked sympathetically, and Agatha would have gone to him if Mr. Cranfield had not restrained her with a speaking look. He was not deceived, and neither was Kitty.

Lord Hatherleigh might enjoy his mirth at her expense now, thought Kitty, but if he believed she was dismayed by such a minor setback, then he did not know her mettle! She mentally rehearsed a scathing setdown, ready to be delivered at a more suitable date.

Two or three minutes later, Lord Hatherleigh emerged from his handkerchief and resumed his former position, valiantly schooling his face into its usual urbane lines with only an occasional spasm.

"Oh, goodness!" Miss Bidwell had been fussing with the baby's smock and now she had it pulled up to expose his ample belly. She looked at Lord Hatherleigh and Kitty as understanding dawned in her clear brown eyes. "So, that is it. My Lord, Miss Whitchurch, have you had the chicken pox?"

"Good God," uttered Kitty in the tone of one receiving a final blow. Her thoughts flew immediately to Sir William. It couldn't be possible... could it?

"So the child is infectious, after all," said the earl, interrupting Kitty's distraught conjectures with the calm statement of fact. "Let me see." Taking Johnny in his arms, he observed the child's chest and stomach and detected the three or four small, pimplelike eruptions which signalled that notoriously contagious disease. Johnny grasped his forefinger during the inspection and held fast.

"You are quite right, Miss Bidwell. Now Mrs. Kimball will know what is the matter and can treat him accordingly." Then, turning to Kitty, the earl demanded, "Well, have you had this particular type of illness, Miss Whitchurch?"

"Yes, of course!" she replied, then added hopefully, "Certainly we all must have had it."

Lord Hatherleigh turned to Agatha and Mr. Cranfield and raised his brows. They both replied to his unspoken question in the affirmative.

"Yes, indeed," added Agatha. "'Twas a nasty business! I shall never forget it!"

"Then the only question remaining is whether Stonebridge has had this unattractive, though usually benign, malady," concluded Lord Hatherleigh in a grave tone. Kitty suspected the depth of that concern, but she could not tell how he looked as his head was bent over Johnny and he was chucking the child under the chin.

"He was an only child," intoned Mr. Cranfield in the mournful tones of an undertaker, "cosseted by his mama till he reached his majority. Before then, whenever anyone so much as sniffled or coughed at Eton or Oxford he was sent home posthaste. With no nieces or nephews, no children of his own and a protective mother, Sir William has perhaps not had the chicken pox."

All eyes turned to Kitty, and each pair conveyed a different emotion. Miss Bidwell's radiated sympathetic concern; Agatha's were fearful; Mr. Cranfield's merely showed a vague, aloof interest, not unlike a scientist's observing a particularly common species of insect. But Kitty braced herself before meeting the one pair of eyes likely to undo her. So it was with great surprise that instead of the expected gleam of triumph, she saw a rather tender twinkle of amusement.

Completely disarmed, Kitty could only say be-musedly, "Poor Sir William. He will be dismayed indeed if that proves true, and he may never forgive me."

"Exactly so." Lord Hatherleigh's voice was so-ber, despite his lips' persistent curve.

SIR WILLIAM HAD NOT had the chicken pox. The news that he might, in one or two weeks, never be able to say so again devastated him. During the first minutes of their trip back through the town he could do naught but mop his brow. He had little to say to anyone, and nothing at all to say to Kitty.

Quite worn out by the events of the day, and knowing herself close to the end of her tether, Kitty leaned back on the luxurious squabs of the carriage and fell silent. Not only was she irritated by the un-fortunate chance of Sir William's exposure to the chicken pox, but she was completely confused by Lord Hatherleigh's reaction. He had made her for-get momentarily how important it was for her to marry Sir William.

What a paradox Lord Hatherleigh was, she thought, glancing over at him and observing that he had tipped the rim of his hat over his eyes and ap-peared to be dozing. One minute sending her into the boughs with his arrogance and conceit, the next minute teasing her with a glimpse of compassion and humour! Why, little Johnny had responded to him quite as readily as Cleopatra! An odd circumstance, considering how offensive the man was!

Then, as if thoughts of one offensive man had power to conjure up another, she saw her cousin Benjamin suddenly gallop into the road. As Kitty gaped in astonishment, he gestured for the coach to stop. Lady Dinwiddie's coachman recognized the honourable Mr. Benjamin Whitchurch, and naturally he reined in the horses. The vehicle rolled to a stop just beside her cousin.

"My dear cousin!" exclaimed Benjamin, halting his own horse and doffing his hat. "How good to see you again!" He looked pointedly at the others and raised his brows.

Kitty had no choice but to introduce him, and she tried to do so without revealing her utter disgust for her relative. She knew he did not look or act the part of a licentious rake. He was as elegantly dressed as usual and doing the pretty in such a way as to make the very best impression. However, when the earl returned his hat to its correct position on his head and leaned over to acknowledge the introduction with the coolest, most abrupt of nods, Benjamin seemed to start, as if suddenly recognizing him.

Kitty found the exchange interesting, but since her cousin recovered quickly and he resumed his manner as before, she dismissed it from her mind.

"Kitty," he was now saying, "I was just at Ridley Hall and found no one there to receive me except Lord Dinwiddie. Dear old fellow that he is, he could not make amends for the absence of my fair cousin and her delightful godmother. And so I told him.'' He chuckled, evidently amused by his own wit and audacity. ''But he said it was of no consequence after all, as I would no doubt see you both at the ball. Then he hastened away on some urgent business with his bailiff. What ball is this, cousin? Are you to have a come-out?''

Kitty forced a lightness to her voice as she answered, ''Well, in a manner of speaking, Benjamin. Lady Dinwiddie so kindly wishes to do it, and I find I am not averse to the idea. It is a pity you cannot come, what with Sarah so recently delivered. I know you cannot wish to attend the ball without her.''

''She wonders why you have not come to see her and little Benjamin,'' he interrupted. ''She's fond of you, y'know.'' He sighed as if hurt for his wife's sake.

Kitty was furious at him for making her appear so unfeeling to the others. She had, in fact, thought often of Sarah and wished to see her, but she had not been able to overcome her repugnance of her cousin in order to make the visit. She flushed and said nothing.

Filling the tense pause that ensued, Miss Bidwell, Agatha and Mr. Cranfield each duly congratulated Benjamin on the birth of his son. Lord Hatherleigh remained silent, as did Sir William, who was too lately disenchanted with baby boys to be able to rejoice in the birth of another.

"You do a disservice to Sarah, though, if you think she would wish to curtail any little enjoyment I might eke out of a country existence, Kitty," Benjamin continued in a moment. "I accept with alacrity your most gracious invitation to attend your ball. I am certain that Sarah would wish it above all things."

Once again Kitty found she had nothing to say, and once again Miss Bidwell charitably filled the awkward pause, this time with a comment on the changeable weather. After two or three other conventional sentences had been exchanged, Benjamin bade them a cheerful farewell and with a triumphant sideways look at Kitty, he rode jauntily away.

CHAPTER FIVE

"It really could not be helped, Godmama. They would escort me. And how should I know little Johnny's fretfulness would turn out to be the chicken pox?" Kitty sat at her dressing table and tried to defend herself, as Lady Dinwiddie deplored her philanthropic activities and their catastrophic result. At the same time, Leah was sternly admonishing her to cease flogging about if she did not wish to look like a positive scarecrow at the dinner table.

"Lord Dinwiddie sets great store by your intelligence, Kitty," fretted Lady Dinwiddie. "He has even gone so far as to call you needle-witted! And until today I have been inclined to agree with him, though I must say it is most unbecoming in a female to be thought of as such. But I wish you had used your head today and kept our guests out of harm's way. You may have had no suspicion that the child's illness would turn out to be the chicken pox, but it could have been many other diseases, equally, if not more serious." Nearly beside herself with exasperation, her ladyship stood behind Kitty's chair wringing her hands.

"Well, I do see your point. I can't think why it did not occur to me," admitted Kitty, frowning at her reflection in the mirror.

"Well, I can imagine!" sniffed Lady Dinwiddie. "You were the healthiest child I have ever had the misfortune to meet. I daresay you do not remember, but when you had the chicken pox I dashed over to nurse you. I was all solicitude and worry but I found you in the top limbs of one of your father's cherry trees! You had hardly any spots and got over it so quickly that I had scarcely anything to do! No wonder you do not think of others falling ill when you have not had any sickness to speak of. And you must know that being so odiously hardy is quite as unbecoming in a female as a preponderance of wit! I wish you may strive, my child, to be a trifle more natural!"

"I realize what a trial I must be to you, dear God-mama," said Kitty demurely, casting her eyes downward to hide the sparkling humour there.

"And of all people, Sir William is the last person in the world to endure with fortitude an attack of the chicken pox. You know how careful he is about his appearance. He cannot wish to wake up one morning covered with spots. It would not surprise me in the least if he should announce himself quite unable to spend another night at Ridley. He could well pack up and be gone before dinner."

"Indeed," replied Kitty in a more serious tone. "I do not think it quite as bad as that. If Sir William did not intend to stay for dinner he would not be shut up with his valet at this very moment having his hair pomaded."

"And, pray, how do you know that?" demanded Lady Dinwiddie.

Kitty glanced at Leah's impassive face and smiled mischievously. "I have my sources."

"Gossiping with the servants, I see! Humph! Well, if he does not go now, surely he will go tomorrow. My lord said he was all in a pucker when you all returned this afternoon!"

"Well, I plan to 'unpucker' the gentleman this evening," declared Kitty, rising to her feet and fluffing the small gathered sleeves of her gown. She was dressed in an elegant creation of richest emerald green. The gown was topped with a fichu of lace in a delicate shade of gold and woven throughout with threads that glimmered and sparkled like fairy dust in the late afternoon light. Her hair was pulled in majestic simplicity away from her face and coiled above in an intricate design. Two full shining ringlets rested on each shoulder.

"Well, my dear!" exclaimed Lady Dinwiddie, much struck by the picture of beauty Kitty revealed when she turned about. "I believe you may! Oh, and do wear that lovely emerald necklace of your mother's. It's so delicately worked that I do not think it will be at all too bold for a girl your age. You must admit that I am not such a stickler for propriety as to be tiresome, am I? You do look lovely!"

"Thank you, Godmama. Let us hope Sir William is as enthusiastic as you are," Kitty said with a chuckle, lifting her ringlets so that Leah might clasp the chain around her neck.

Lady Dinwiddie looked shrewd. "Ah, you do have serious designs on the gentleman, don't you, my dear? I hoped you would realize the great good sense of fixing your interest on Sir William. I am glad you are not merely trying to pacify me. How clever of you to take advantage of this visit and not wait for a trip to London to try your luck. As they say, 'A bird in the hand is worth two in the tree!' Or is it 'in the shrub...?'"

Kitty coloured a little at her godmother's forthright representation of things, but could not deny the truth of it. "It's two in the bush, Godmama," she supplied.

"What a relief it is that you are not a silly romantical miss!" she continued, patting Kitty's flushed cheeks affectionately. "And to reward you for being such a good and clever godchild, Katherine, and if the skies do not bode ill in the morning, we will go on our expedition!" Lady Dinwiddie walked to the window and frowned up at the sky. "What was it Sir William was saying about wishing to see you amongst the summer blooms? Well, we shall just have to give him the chance.... Oh! Look, Katherine. There's Lord Hatherleigh, just returning from a ride! Can you imagine? With less than half an hour left to dress for dinner! But he is never late. La, what a good seat he has on that white stallion of his! Gone 'round to the stables now.... Well, I had best be going downstairs. Miss Bidwell and Mr. Cranfield are always the first to assemble in the drawing room and heaven knows what they may find to say to each other! Are you coming, Katherine?''

Kitty had joined Lady Dinwiddie at the window. ''No. I want to sit quietly for a few minutes. I'll be down directly.''

''As you wish, but don't dawdle too long, as time is of the essence in this situation. You had better use each moment to your advantage,'' Lady Dinwiddie earnestly admonished her.

Kitty nodded absentmindedly and Lady Dinwiddie left. Kitty turned back to the window just as Lord Hatherleigh strode onto the gravel drive from the back of the house. She stepped behind the curtains and watched his progress to the door.

She could not help a small smile. He did not require an inordinate amount of time to make himself presentable for dinner, and no one could ever find fault with his well-groomed, impeccable appearance. Even now, in his buckskin breeches and high-topped riding boots, he was the perfect image of what a man should be.

Entirely forgetting her intention to sit quietly for a time, Kitty stood as if in a trance, and watched with no thoughts beyond her involuntary and spontaneous admiration of one who had such a perverse talent for irritating her beyond bearing. But who, she thought, could not admire the broad shoulders, the lithe firmness of his figure and the seemingly effortless agility of his movements? He was close enough now for her to appreciate the heightened colour of his complexion due to his recent exercise. He looked so vibrant and alive, the picture of healthy, energetic manhood....

When he disappeared beneath the overhanging façade of the house, Kitty guiltily collected her wandering thoughts and went back to the reality of the conversation with her godmother. "It certainly *is* fortunate that I am not a silly, romantical miss," she whispered with amused self-derision, then sighed softly into the velvet folds of Lady Dinwiddie's draperies.

Cleopatra, who had been napping peacefully on the bed, jumped down and gained Kitty's immediate attention by rubbing against her skirt.

"You troublesome creature," Kitty said, laughing, picking up her plump pet and moving towards the door. "Leah will have your hide if you persist in depositing hair on my gown! Come, girl," she continued, lifting her chin determinedly. "Let's show Lord Hatherleigh just what a little country chit can do!" She set Cleopatra on the floor and they both strode with great dignity from the room.

In an effort to entertain her guests, Lady Dinwiddie had invited the local vicar, his wife, two sons and a daughter to dinner. The two young men were down from Oxford, well grown and good-looking in a wholesome country way, and though a year separated them in birth, they were so similar in looks as to be frequently mistaken for twins. Since their stay away from home had partially cured them of their natural shyness, they looked forward to the social gathering at the Dinwiddies' with happy anticipation. This expectation of pleasure was not, however, based on the hope of seeing Kitty or any other young woman, but on the sure knowledge that Lord Dinwiddie owned a very handsome billiard table.

At the blooming age of seventeen the rector's daughter, Patience, was held to be quite pretty. She was also of an uncommonly serious tone of mind. Lord Dinwiddie had quizzed his wife about it that morning, hinting that she must be up to her matchmaking tricks again. Lady Dinwiddie airily disclaimed any such motives, but Lord Dinwiddie said that she needn't try to take him for a gudgeon because it was obvious she meant Patience for Cedric Cranfield.

"Well, and don't you think they should exactly suit, Arthur? With their fair hair and sober countenance, they would look so well together. Like two bookends! Besides, with her upbringing she'd be the perfect clergyman's wife!"

"That would depend entirely upon the clergyman in question, my dear. Besides, Cranfield's eggs are in a different basket altogether."

"What did you say, dear? Well, never mind. I must speak with Cook about the veal in...in...well, you know, that French sauce she makes! It was a trifle salty last time, and so I told her most forcefully! I thought I should sink when Lord Stavely declined a second serving. He never does, you know!''

"I am persuaded that Cook will have taken your remonstrations to heart, my dear," said Lord Dinwiddie reassuringly, "and tonight's dinner will be all that you, or the fastidious Lord Stavely, might wish for. However, as it is the simple palate of the Reverend Howard that we must please and not Lord Stavely's, I really see no cause for concern."

As always, Lord Dinwiddie's felicitous predictions for the evening's meal were correct. No one could have found the least fault with any of the numerous dishes and side dishes offered them.

Despite his epicurean tendencies, Sir William grew positively indifferent to his steamed artichokes when confronted with the beautiful and agreeable Miss Whitchurch. He had come down with only a few minutes to spare, a distinctly discontented expression on his face. His gaze, however, had become immediately riveted on that young lady. Silhouetted against the white marble mantelpiece, in a regal green gown which exactly matched her eyes, her hands folded so delicately in her lap, she had looked up and smiled so welcomingly that he instantly found himself distracted. He got through the introductions and had a vague idea of a respectable couple, two tall young men—or was he seeing double?—and a pretty girl with a very solemn expression.

Then, he did not know exactly how it came about, but Lord Hatherleigh was suddenly before him as he turned back to Miss Whitchurch. The earl blocked his view entirely and was now engaging him in the most banal conversation! And, just as he hoped to extricate himself and proceed to the vacant chair by Miss Whitchurch, Lord Hatherleigh took his arm and led him to the quiet corner where Miss Bidwell sat composedly alone. Miss Bidwell had told his lordship of a most interesting volume she had recently perused. It was, Lord Hatherleigh declared, exactly that sort of work to enthrall Sir William. He was sure Miss Bidwell would be delighted to repeat her observations.

Sir William was not a great reader—in fact he hardly ever turned a page!—but politeness demanded he respond with a show of enthusiasm. He sat down reluctantly and, after exchanging a few civil sentences with Miss Bidwell, looked up to find Lord Hatherleigh gone and in possession of the very seat by Miss Whitchurch he himself had meant to occupy.

Kitty saw it all, but hid her vexation from the general view, only allowing herself to lean towards Lord Hatherleigh and between smiling teeth hiss a most unflattering description of his character.

Lord Hatherleigh bore this critique very well, and smilingly replied, "Perhaps you are correct, Miss Whitchurch. But though my behaviour is reprehensible, the results are indisputable. Sir William was irritated with me at first—how could it be otherwise with such a vision as yourself before him?—but now, you see, he is quite engrossed with Miss Bidwell."

Kitty turned to the couple and saw them engaged in what, by all appearances, was indeed a very absorbing conversation. Under normal circumstances, she could never wish to curtail Miss Bidwell's enjoyment but tonight she had no desire to share Sir William with anyone. She knew she had work to do. He was undoubtedly still in need of mollifying after his traumatic experience at the Kimballs'.

But at last they were at table and there Lord Hatherleigh could not usurp Sir William's place. With him securely seated beside her, Kitty gave full rein to every charm and wile she possessed.

It was at this point, over the aforementioned cooling artichoke, that Sir William was compelled to say, "My dear Miss Whitchurch, allow me to say I have never seen you in such looks! And after such a demanding task as you performed this morning! I wonder at your looking so fresh!"

"Indeed, Sir William," replied Kitty, her face expressing great solicitude. "I was loath to mention it, but since you do, I must tell you how much I feel on your account! Had I known, I would never have exposed you to such dangers. And you with such a delicate constitution as I am persuaded you possess! You must know your welfare is of the utmost importance—" She stopped abruptly and looked very self-conscious.

Sir William took this maidenly expression of concern just as Kitty had intended. He was very pleased and, patting her hand, gently reassured her. "There, there, my dear. Do not trouble yourself. You were led into indiscretion by your zeal for good works...your innate goodness! I admit to being a bit dismayed earlier by the results, but I feel much less alarm now. Miss Bidwell has so kindly educated me—and in the most minute terms!—concerning the precise nature of the illness, and has assured me that she should be glad to apply her extensive experience with the disease should I indeed develop it. And she is by no means convinced that I shall! I own I had considered leaving tomorrow, though I detest the thought of removing myself from your radiant presence, but she assures me that that would be unnecessary. Furthermore, she says I must not mope about, as that would reduce my ability to resist the disease, but must go on exactly as before! I was not sure I believed her at first, you know, but just the way she said it, in such a certain though kind accent, I was quite reminded of my mother...."

And so Sir William went on, detailing every little fact he had learned from Miss Bidwell, including vivid anecdotes of each of her brothers' slightly varying reactions and a complete account of the ministrations of her mother and herself. Such a narrative could not have been anything but extremely tedious to Kitty, but she attended with all the appearance of interest. The repetition of his conversation with Miss Bidwell seemed to make him happy, and Kitty was determined to please him. She was amazed that Miss Bidwell had had the patience to relate and explain all this in the first place, but was thankful that she had been available to do so. Certainly Kitty, who had little experience of nursing, would not have reassured him so effectively.

Several minutes and two courses later, when Sir William had finished his monologue, Kitty ventured to mention the outing planned for the following day. "I am so glad you are staying, Sir William, for tomorrow we go to see the abbey ruins. You do mean to attend us?"

Kitty really did look forward to the outing and was rather anxious for his reply. She hoped she would not be obliged to sit home with him and play piquet.

"If I do not exert myself unnecessarily, I daresay I shall be equal to it," he answered. Kitty smiled her approbation so charmingly that Sir William had appetite for only half of his veal, and though Lady Dinwiddie noticed his restraint, she did not repine. She rightly attributed Sir Williams's disinterest in the veal to an increased interest in her goddaughter.

After dinner, when what they considered a reasonable space of time had passed, the two young men from the vicarage alluded in an offhand manner to Lord Dinwiddie's bang-up-to-the-mark billiard table. Lord Dinwiddie took the hint, and after enquiring of his wife if she had definite plans for cards or duets and receiving a good-natured negative, he invited everyone into the games room, where the billiard table dominated its surroundings.

"Do you care to play, Miss Whitchurch?" asked Sir William.

"No, but I shall be pleased to watch," replied Kitty with a coy smile.

Much gratified, he offered his arm and led her out of the drawing room and into the games room. The group assembled there much as Kitty might have anticipated. Lord Hatherleigh bent over the billiard table, testing his stick while Agatha stood at his elbow chattering like a magpie, seemingly unmoved that he did not attend to her in the least. The young Messrs. Howard likewise stood by the table watching Lord Hatherleigh, whom they had heard was a noted Corinthian, and tried to imitate his stance. Kitty noted that, to his credit, he answered the frequent questions addressed to him by the admiring duo with good-humoured tolerance.

Lord and Lady Dinwiddie, Lady Cranfield and the Howards sat in a circle, a situation they deemed most convenient for gossiping. Teresa Bidwell sat in a chair by the fireplace and took up her work box. When asked if he cared to join, Mr. Cranfield announced regretfully that he found billiards to be a complete waste of time, but could, however, imagine the fascination it might hold for others. He deigned to watch the progress of the game but it was from a distant chair and with a faintly contemptuous eye.

Employing gentle nudges and a constant flow of conversation, Lady Dinwiddie had tried to deposit Patience Howard in a chair by Mr. Cranfield, but she was not to have her way. Having sat by the fair Patience at dinner, and having no deficiency of understanding, Mr. Cranfield divined what Lady Dinwiddie was about and frowned forbiddingly. He need not have worried, however, because Patience, blessed equally with understanding, coolly but firmly asserted her wish to occupy one of the two vacant seats by Miss Bidwell. Kitty watched all this with great amusement and concluded that Lady Dinwiddie was not always fortunate in her matchmaking attempts.

"You must stand by the table, Miss Whitchurch, or I shall have no luck at all," cried Sir William when Kitty also seemed likely to join Teresa.

"If you insist," she began, but was interrupted by Lord Hatherleigh, who intoned laconically, "I insist that there be no ladies at the table." Then, as everyone looked startled at this rather rude statement, he softened it considerably with a small, crooked smile, "Beauty and charm are always a distraction."

Sir William shrugged his well-padded shoulders apologetically at Kitty, while Agatha laughed uneasily and mumbled something about how droll dear Nathan was. Then she quickly claimed the other vacant chair by Teresa. Kitty had no recourse but to sit by Mr. Cranfield. She was irritated by the earl's dismissal of her from the table, but short of creating a scene she saw that there was nothing to be done about it. She resigned herself to watching in silence, but after five minutes she was surprised by signs of life in her companion. He was clicking his tongue as if quite disgusted about something.

"What is it, Mr. Cranfield?" questioned Kitty curiously. She thought it must be something really dreadful for the gentleman to be actually displaying his displeasure in such a way.

"I beg your pardon, Miss Whitchurch?" He turned to her with a preoccupied air.

"Is something wrong? I thought I heard...no, I am quite certain I heard you 'tsk' just now."

"Tsk?" His brows lowered and his lips pursed as if genuinely puzzled by her observation. "No, no," he finally concluded broodingly, "you must have heard the clock ticking." He turned again and stared in the direction of the others.

A little out of temper owing to the strain of playing the besotted maiden, Kitty was about to retort that she was not such a ninny-hammer as to mistake a tick for a "tsk." But she thought better of it and picked up a book from the gleaming surface of a cherry wood table next to her chair. It was *A Sicilian Romance* by Mrs. Radcliffe, and Kitty began to read.

Another five minutes passed and she heard the sound again. Mr. Cranfield was "tsk-tsking" and dolefully shaking his head, as well.

"Mr. Cranfield!" exclaimed Kitty, both amused and exasperated. "You evidently find that something is amiss!" She glanced around, wondering if the cause of his disgruntlement could be Lady Cranfield's petticoat, which hung two inches below her ruffled hem when she sat down, or if Sir Williams's shirt points, so high that they kept him from comfortably turning his head, had drawn her companion's censure. She had to admit that Sir William did pose rather oddly when he lined up his ball.

"Miss Whitchurch," Mr. Cranfield insisted icily, "nothing is amiss." Despite his quelling tone, Kitty observed that he had turned absolutely red, and though he darted a quick glance at her, he immediately returned his fixed gaze to the group nearest the billiard table. This only piqued Kitty's curiosity further and she determined to provoke him into telling her the truth.

"Why, I can think of no reason for you to be so displeased unless you find fault with someone or with their manner of dress. As a man of the cloth, Mr. Cranfield, surely you must understand the importance of tolerance for these foibles of others, however silly you might find them."

"Miss Whitchurch!" he exclaimed, becoming an even deeper shade of crimson and finally turning to allow her his complete attention. "They might all be in monks' robes for all I care! And if you must know, I am simply a little dismayed to see that Agatha still has not completely recovered from his lordship's latest stinging set-down!''

Kitty's eyes flew to where Agatha sat. Agatha was not engaged in her usual animated conversation. Instead, she seemed deeply engrossed in smoothing nonexistent wrinkles from her delicate silken gown, and though her head was bent, Kitty could see enough of her face to realize that Agatha did look a little depressed.

''Mr. Cranfield,'' pursued Kitty, ''surely you do not imply that his lordship behaves badly towards his intended bride? I admit to noticing a kind of patronizing attitude at times, but never to the point of absolute rudeness or unkindness.''

''Did you not observe his dismissal of her from the table just now?'' he asked with asperity.

''Yes, but he did not refer just to Agatha. He meant me, as well! And he did try to sweeten it up a bit with that contrived compliment about beauty and charm.''

''If it were an isolated incident,'' he explained in a patient voice, as if instructing a very dull pupil, ''it would be nothing, of course. But that is not the case. He is rarely, as you put it, absolutely rude, but he is continually negligent in his attitude towards Agatha, and though she is a trifle featherbrained, she is not so short in the sheet that she does not feel it.''

''Then why does she not simply terminate the engagement? If I did not like the way I was treated, that is what I should do!''

"Well, that is not what Agatha should do." He sighed deeply. "Hatherleigh is considered the most eligible bachelor in England. He is wealthy and titled, and not bad-looking as they go...but even if Agatha didn't care a fig for the fellow, with her Mama fairly drooling over him and all her friends congratulating her upon her great good luck, she cannot help but have convinced herself that it is a most desirable connection."

Kitty could hardly believe she was having this conversation with Mr. Cranfield. She had always found him close-mouthed to the point of incivility before, and she could only conclude that his feelings were now too strong and had led him, against his better judgement, to speak freely with her. But what exactly was the nature of those feelings? Suddenly it seemed very important that she know the answer to this question. Fearing a return to his previous taciturnity, Kitty pressed on.

"But if what you say of the earl is true, surely he could wed anyone in England he chose. If he does not care for Agatha, why should he have asked her to marry him?"

"Ah, that is a good question." He glanced at her briefly and smiled tightly, then returned his gaze to Agatha. "But I have an equally excellent answer for you. It has been his mother's and my stepmother's dearest wish to unite their children in marriage. They have planned it since their nursery days. Their mothers are bosom-bows and their estates march together, you know."

"No, I did not know!" Kitty exclaimed with interest. "I wonder Lady Dinwiddie did not tell me all this. Then there was more inducement for the union than Agatha's considerable beauty."

"Yes, but though it seemed foreordained, it was not until the conclusion of Agatha's second season that Hatherleigh came up to scratch. My dear stepmother was quite beside herself. She had turned away some very eligible suitors in expectation of Hatherleigh's offer. Since the engagement, as you can well imagine, her cup runneth over."

Kitty fell silent. She watched Mr. Cranfield watch Agatha. He was in love with her, that was obvious. And why it had not occurred to Kitty before, she could not say.

She looked at Agatha, who was finally responding to Teresa's gentle attempts at conversation. Agatha laughed, and turning back to Mr. Cranfield, Kitty observed the softening of his eyes and the slight upturning of his stern mouth. Ah, this is what love can do, she mused. Agatha's pretty, childlike ingenuousness had found a space in Mr. Cranfield's staid heart, had nestled comfortably there and finally blossomed into love. But how sad. This love was destined to be unrequited.

Kitty began to feel uncomfortable. She had never regarded love affairs of others so sentimentally before. She found she was deeply moved by the fact that Mr. Cranfield would be denied fulfillment of a love that could very well have softened the hard edges of his vigilant, rigid approach to life and might well have made him a truly happy human being. As for Agatha...

Kitty turned to watch Lord Hatherleigh at the billiard table. His full profile was in view as he leaned over the table and carefully lined up his cue for the next point. The strong muscles of his thighs pulled against the material of his pantaloons. His broad back and shoulders strained slightly beneath his well-cut coat, and his strong, slender fingers cradled the stick with expert ease. She was reminded of the feel of those strong fingers on her back the night he'd kissed her. And the kiss was hard to forget, too.

Kitty sighed. Unlike her, Agatha was definitely a romantical young woman, and if she could be content merely to bask in the reflected glow of Lord Hatherleigh's popularity, or even—Kitty blushed at the thought—to thrill at his touch, perhaps there was a chance for her happiness. But Kitty strongly doubted this. As she studied the young lady she realized that Agatha needed abiding affection and respect. And despite Lord Hatherleigh's possible good intentions, he appeared to cherish neither of these emotions where Agatha was concerned.

Being a creature of action and decision, Kitty immediately set about planning how she might separate Agatha from Lord Hatherleigh and join her with Mr. Cranfield. It was an absorbing topic, and she had to be called twice by Sir William before her attention was caught. She looked up guiltily and listened as he explained the marvelous shot he'd just executed. Kitty smiled graciously, and Sir William resumed the game. But Lord Hatherleigh was at leisure to look where he pleased, and he chose to look at Kitty. He smiled and winked, and Kitty blushed hotly. If he only knew what she had been plotting, he'd as soon wring her neck as smile at her.

My, but she would be a busy girl tomorrow! She must do some matchmaking for Agatha as well as herself, and she was certain that the majority of the people present in the room would not view her activities with benevolence. But do them she must.

CHAPTER SIX

THE NEXT MORNING, as they gathered in the drawing room for the abbey expedition, the eager party was greeted with the news that Lady Cranfield was suffering a slight indisposition and would not be joining them. Kitty suspected that the noble lady's nonappearance was due more to a dislike of eating out-of-doors without the benefit of numerous servants and a stout table than to any infirmity of health. A sideboard groaning beneath several courses and large padded chairs to support her ample girth were undoubtedly much more to her ladyship's taste. Regardless of the reasons for Lady Cranfield's refusal, however, Miss Bidwell charitably offered to remain behind and partner her in a game or two of whist.

As there would be seven of them—eight if Cleopatra could be counted—Lady Dinwiddie proposed that they take the large and more commodious barouche. That way, she said, they could be all together for the short trip and have a comfortable coze on the way. Despite the outward vivacity of the group, Kitty sensed a certain tension between some of its members. Mr. Cranfield had grown quite cool toward her as he was evidently regretting his confessions of the night before. Agatha was talking rather more than usual, in a frenzied kind of way, and Sir William had been made a trifle nervous by Lady Cranfield's supposed indisposition.

Kitty was glad when they arrived at their destination and, ignoring Sir William's proffered hand, alighted from the carriage with a bounce that reflected her happiness to be outdoors, but which however, drew a disapproving frown from Lady Dinwiddie.

The party found a large oak tree near a lovely stream, spread their blankets and looked at the baskets of food brought forth with evident eagerness. Lady Dinwiddie was in her element, making sure everyone had plenty to eat, and insisting with every plate of food she passed around that there was nothing like fresh air to whet the appetite.

Luncheon completed, the abbey ruins beckoned, and Kitty stood up, replaced her discarded bonnet on her head and was ready to lead the way.

"I hope you do not mind, Miss Whitchurch," came Sir William's rather subdued voice from the blanket where he half-reclined. "I find I am not up to a walk just now. I think I had rather rest. I would not wish to overexert myself just at this critical point, you know." He stifled a yawn and smiled dreamily up at her. "You may stay with me, if you wish."

The invitation had undoubtedly been prompted by the ludicrous way in which Kitty's face fell when Sir

William announced his intention to stay behind. He thought she was dismayed at the loss of his company. Actually she was overcome because she knew she ought to stay behind and spend her afternoon flirting instead of sight-seeing. Lady Dinwiddie would not object because in such casual circumstances a chaperon would not be considered strictly necessary. Besides, Jed the coachman would be nearby.

But Kitty had been looking forward to this outing and restrained a strong urge to stamp her foot and fly into a rage not unlike a two-year-old. A vision of Lord Hatherleigh leading Jezebel away presently restored her composure and her lips stretched into a smile, despite her teeth's tendency to grind together in frustration.

"But of course, Sir William, I should be delighted." She resettled herself on the blanket while the others walked away. Lagging behind, Lord Hatherleigh turned and, ascertaining that Sir William was occupied in settling his head against a convenient tree root, winked again and smiled. Kitty raised her brows haughtily and turned back to Sir William.

She resigned herself to her fate and determined to make the most of it. To her chagrin, her would-be lover had closed his eyes and looked well on his way to deep slumber. Kitty sighed and philosophically decided that since Sir William obviously would not appreciate conversation right now, she might as well enjoy her peaceful surroundings.

Sardonically regarding the ardent lover, the coachman decided that Kitty was in no immediate danger of being ravaged. He excused himself and wandered downstream, seeking a comfortable resting place of his own for a snooze.

Kitty smiled him away, then sat quietly for a few minutes stroking Cleopatra, who was nestled in her lap, and contemplated the clear water's silvery path over the rocks and pieces of wood that had lodged along the banks of the stream. She delighted in the tiny cascades created by the different heights and depths of the stream bed, and the gently rushing noise of the moving water soothed her agitated mind. Had she had a comfortable prop for her head she might have fallen asleep as well, but she was shaken rather suddenly out of her reverie by the sound of Cleopatra's piteous but determined meow. She had not noticed that her pet had vacated her lap, but she had indeed, and was now huddled against the trunk of a tree whose branches stretched out over the water. Unfortunately she was several boughs up, at least twelve feet above the ground.

"Cleopatra!" admonished Kitty in a vehement whisper as she stood up, shook out the skirts of her royal blue walking dress and strode impatiently to the tree.

"You are not a kitten any longer and I cannot abide this ridiculous obsession you have for climbing trees! If you could descend just as quickly and easily as you got up, I should not mind! But we both know that this is not the case!'' She paused and frowned up at her recalcitrant pet, who shifted uneasily on her perch and looked down pleadingly. Kitty sighed with exasperation.

"As always you expect me to rescue you,'' she muttered. She glanced over at Sir William's reclining figure and saw that the gentleman was indeed unconscious, his mouth sagging open and his chin quivering with each intake of breath. He would have been shocked at the unflattering spectacle he presented, but Kitty was grateful for his complete absorption in Morpheus' world. She felt free to pursue the necessary course of action.

Hiking her fashionably narrow skirt well above her knees and kicking off her shoes, she proceeded to climb the tree. She did so quickly as she had had considerable experience in the art. She had just reached Cleopatra when she was startled into immobility by a quiet, amused voice from the bottom of the tree.

"My dear Miss Whitchurch! I had not expected this...even from you!''

Kitty was well aware that she was showing a good deal of leg as she looked down into the grinning face of Lord Hatherleigh, and blushed profusely.

"You...you...!'' she stammered, her eyes frantically darting to Sir William. "If you do not turn your face this instant, as any gentleman would have done without being told, I shall take great pleasure in slapping you when once I am down!"

"As you wish, madam" was his solemn reply, belied however by the gleam in his eyes as he obediently turned away.

Kitty rather urgently grabbed her pet and hastily and awkwardly climbed down. She dumped Cleopatra unceremoniously on the grass, pulled her skirt into place and glared at the earl's broad back, her chest heaving with emotion.

Observing Cleopatra sauntering past, the earl turned about and looked at Kitty. He was amused but as calm and unperturbed as ever. "I assume it is safe to look now?"

"What are you doing here?" demanded Kitty in a fierce whisper. "Why are you forever where I do not wish you to be?"

"Miss Whitchurch, I can readily explain. Agatha sent me to fetch her parasol—you recollect, the one she was so taken with in Trumpington the other day? Lord Dinwiddie was not equal to the exertion, nor was Cranfield willing to leave Agatha for so long a time, so I, ever the compliant fiancé, hastened back to fetch it. Her complexion is decidedly delicate...."

"Do please lower your voice," admonished Kitty, glancing nervously toward Sir William, who had rolled over onto his side with a loud snort.

"Oh, he won't wake up," the earl casually reassured her. "He has a nap every day, you know.

Nothing short of a cannon's roar could disturb Sir William once he's dozed off.''

"And why should I believe you? You would like nothing better than to sink me in his eyes!'' Kitty argued.

"Why are you worried? Granted, if he'd seen you in the tree as I just did . . . On the other hand, perhaps he'd feel more disposed to marry you if he'd seen what charming limbs you have.''

"It's very ungentlemanly of you to remind me of it,'' Kitty declared petulantly, stooping to retrieve her shoes. "I am mortified! You are unfeeling in the extreme!'' Much to Kitty's surprise her voice cracked and her eyes traitorously filled with tears. She was indeed mortified! It did pain her to have so fully lived up to his idea of her as a hoydenish, silly, country chit!

She flopped to the ground and tugged her shoes on, pulling her skirt carefully down and making sure that not even a hint of ankle was exposed. How she wished she'd never entered into a wager with the earl! He'd called it a most imprudent wager, and she was beginning to agree with him. Not only was it spoiling all her fun, but she was continually having to fence with him—and he always won! She was so unaccountably out of control and so near bursting into tears that she didn't dare look up at him. She wrapped her arms protectively around her knees and stared at the ground.

"Come, my dear. It's not as bad as all that. Why, if you only knew how many knees I've seen in my day... Hmm, well, perhaps that isn't the best way to approach it...."

Taken by surprise at the sympathetic tone of his voice, devoid of any mocking sarcasm, Kitty looked up. Lord Hatherleigh surveyed her intently and his thumb and forefinger caressed his chin thoughtfully.

"Are you trying to apologize to me again, Lord Hatherleigh?" Kitty questioned cautiously.

"It is a shame I am forced to do so again, isn't it? But you're such a game bit of a girl—pluck to the backbone as they say!—that I find it exhilarating to match wits with you. But I've gone too far and brought tears to your eyes this time. I beg your pardon." He reached forth a hand to help her up.

"I am not crying," she insisted, turning her head sharply to the right.

"Not yet, but I see the tears shining in your eyes. One blink of your lashes will bring them spilling over. Don't be embarrassed. I find it refreshing to see a young woman valiantly trying to suppress tears instead of using them to get her way. Come! Get up!" he demanded in a rallying voice. "Even Sir Will may wake up if we continue to squabble, and even now Agatha's skin may be scorched to an unflattering shade of brown!"

Since a blink of her lashes had brought forth the predicted tears, Kitty tried to whisk them away with the back of her hand before allowing Lord Hatherleigh to take both her hands in his and pull her to her feet. Once in an upright position she found herself not twelve inches away from that gentleman. Though she was a tall girl, she still had to tilt her head back to look into his face.

What she saw there was disconcerting in the extreme. Tenderness softened the sardonic lines of his mouth and humour and warmth kindled his eyes to a brilliant shade of blue. Coming unbidden to her mind was the memory of his kiss. It had been a mocking kiss, pressed on her unwillingly and taken by him without a serious thought. Now that he knew her, would a kiss feel different? she wondered. He was kind sometimes. He was being kind to her now, and she felt herself leaning ever so slightly forward.

Lord Hatherleigh abruptly dropped her hands and turned away. "Now where is that confounded parasol?" He wandered away towards the carriage.

Kitty swayed slightly, blinking several times in a dazed sort of way, effectively emptying her eyes of the rest of the unwanted tears. She'd dried her cheeks by the time the earl had found the parasol and was prepared to meet his gaze when he returned. She felt sure she'd made an utter fool of herself and in an attempt to salvage the situation somehow was compelled to take advantage of his charitable mood by asking, "Why aren't you kinder to Agatha?"

"What did you say?" The earl seemed struck motionless, his voice forbiddingly low and clipped.

"I said," Kitty persisted, her chin thrust forward bravely, "why do you not treat Agatha more kindly? You can be kind."

"Well, it is very generous of you to say so, Miss Whitchurch," he returned with his usual sarcasm. "But as you are so apt to tell me, it is none of your affair. If Agatha has a complaint about the way I treat her, she ought to come to me instead of prattling away to a girl friend."

"She did not prattle away to me!"

"Then why do you raise such a question? I am not aware that I have done or said anything to discompose Agatha."

"Indeed, I don't suppose you are!" cried Kitty. "To your credit I believe your rudeness is completely unintentional!"

"My rudeness! Why, you little slip of a female! How dare you..."

"You are acting quite guilty now, you know. You would not react so heatedly if you did not recognize some truth in what I say!"

This time it was the earl's turn to blink. He seemed astonished and deeply affected by Kitty's words. His eyes glittered intensely, and Kitty was afraid he meant to box her ears as Leah had done to her when she was a child and had overstepped her bounds. He struggled with whatever emotion held him in such a harsh grip, pressed his lips together so tightly as to turn them white at the edges, and tapped the top of his boot with Agatha's parasol for such a length of time that Kitty began to tremble.

Just when she felt as though she might sink under the weight of the tension, a strident scream resounded in the distance. The volume and the pitch of the sound was so terrifying that even Sir William woke up, midsnore, to exclaim, "Good heavens, what on earth was that?"

Kitty tried to keep up with Lord Hatherleigh, who had begun to run at the first sound of the scream. Skirting the edge of the stream bank, pushing back the encroaching tree limbs and bushes with a forceful swing of his arm, Lord Hatherleigh swiftly arrived at the scene of the upheaval. Kitty arrived a moment later. Her hair flew untidily about her face and the several leaves deposited in its glossy waves testified to her own haste. Casting her eyes about for blood or any sign of catastrophe, Kitty was relieved to see nothing of the sort. There was only Agatha, lying limp and pale in Mr. Cranfield's arms. She had fainted.

"What the devil has happened here?" growled the earl.

"A snake! An enormous, terrifying snake!" Lady Dinwiddie moaned faintly, propped up against her husband and breathing rapidly.

"It was only a grass snake," Lord Dinwiddie assured Hatherleigh with an exasperated shake of his head. "But you know how the ladies are about anything that slithers. Agatha was the first to see it."

"Where is it now?" questioned the earl with a relieved sigh.

"Over there somewhere." Lady Dinwiddie motioned weakly with her handkerchief.

"Do you have any hartshorn, Godmama?" asked Kitty, observing Agatha's white face and feeling that something should be done to revive her. She looked up at Mr. Cranfield and was startled to find him as white as his stepsister.

"In my reticule. In the carriage."

"At any rate, it is better that she does not revive until we reach the carriage," Lord Hatherleigh stated grimly, gently lifting his fiancée out of Mr. Cranfield's arms and setting out for the carriage. "If the snake were to make an encore appearance she might go into another swoon."

"What has happened? What is amiss?" Sir William's harassed countenance appeared from behind a nearby bush. He was huffing and puffing with the unusual exertion of having run through the woods.

"There was a..."

The disclosure was unnecessary. Sir William had stepped directly onto the unsuspecting and undoubtedly frightened reptile. It gave a convulsive wriggle and vanished, but it had scared Sir William half out of his wits. He let out a scream not unworthy of Agatha's earlier performance and backed away to the very edge of the stream.

"Oh, Sir William, do pray step forward!" exclaimed Kitty, but it was too late. Arms flung high and wide and circling vigorously, Sir William hit the water with a resounding slap. Mr. Cranfield jumped in to save Sir William from flogging himself senseless as he struggled in the scant eighteen inches of water warbling pleasantly around him. Wet and chilled to the bone, Sir William was dazedly pulled from the stream. Mr. Cranfield took a firm grip on his arm and led him back to the group.

What a grim spectacle, thought Kitty, as she walked behind the dripping, drooping entourage. She carried the discarded parasol, Agatha's bonnet and Sir William's soggy neckcloth. Lord Hatherleigh led the party, carrying a still-insensible Agatha, Mr. Cranfield followed with Sir William in tow, and Lord and Lady Dinwiddie walked just ahead of her at the excruciatingly slow pace necessary when one person entirely supported the weight of the other. Perhaps she would not soon wish for another outing to the abbey ruins, she thought, brushing a leaf from her hair.

THE BALL WAS PUT OFF for a week in the hope that Sir William would recover sufficiently to attend. Dr. Rutherford had insisted that Sir William not remove from Ridley Hall. Though he had merely caught a cold and his physical sufferings were minimal, his nerves were in a state of profound agitation. He was carefully conveyed to the grand suite on the upper floor, which had an attached private parlour. He sat in there when he was feeling up to it and received visitors.

Kitty dropped in frequently, but could force herself to stay only a very few moments. Sir William had become so used to being mollycoddled by his mother and his late wife, he had been so encouraged to speak endlessly of every slight discomfort, that he was a most tiresome companion. Many times Kitty regretted the wager she had entered into with Lord Hatherleigh. She had made a terrible mistake.

Her assumptions about the matrimonial state were undergoing daily changes. She had thought it would be easy to adapt to someone, to live with him, even to bear his children. She had not thought it would require so much effort. She had been a fool, she glumly admitted. Perhaps there was something to this thing called "romantic love," after all.

But if she did not get out of her wager with the earl she would either have to press forward in her bid to marry Sir William, or lose her horse. She wished beyond anything to be released of the odious word of honour and to be free to explore the new ideas that had recently been disrupting her former practical views of the married state.

As the days passed, Kitty observed with awe the charitable extent to which Miss Bidwell catered to Sir William's sickly whims. Teresa's patience and forbearance when he whined on about something Kitty could only scoff at earned her utmost admiration. She had never considered herself unfeeling, but she found that her sympathy had limits, while Miss Bidwell's appeared boundless, indeed.

Kitty had sympathy enough for Mr. Cranfield, however. Though it would seem to be a desirable reversal, the earl's suddenly punctilious, constant good manners and kindness to his fiancée did not delight Mr. Cranfield. Kitty's words to the earl had evidently been taken to heart, but in Mr. Cranfield they provoked only jealousy.

Agatha herself appeared bewildered and occasionally looked at her fiancé as though he had lost his mind. He was not loverlike or overly fawning—that would have disgusted Kitty!—but his manners were so improved towards Agatha that she wondered her words could have wrought such a change in the man. But she wondered still more why his attentions to Agatha should disturb her quite as much as they did Mr. Cranfield. There could no longer be any necessity to rescue Agatha from marriage to the earl, and Mr. Cranfield had to accept the inevitable.

Preparations went forth for the ball, and Cook and Mrs. Wells were grateful for the additional time given them. Miss Beaufort created a stunning gown for Kitty, and it was one afternoon as Kitty stood for a fitting that Lady Dinwiddie peeked around the door of her bedchamber to say, "Katherine, where have you been for the past hour? Surely not here, because I've had the servants check on you time and again!"

"I was walking by the lake, Godmama, and I came directly to my room afterwards and found Miss Beaufort wishing me to stand for a fitting. I did not know you sought me."

"Well, never mind. You'll never guess who has called! It is Sarah! Sarah has come to visit and it was just yesterday that Benjamin claimed her to be still as weak as a kitten after her lying-in! What can the man be about? Do come down! She wishes particularly to see you and has been sitting with me this past hour in the hope you would appear!"

Kitty hurried into a light summer dress and descended the stairs full of curiosity. She and Lady Dinwiddie had made a visit to Sarah shortly after encountering Benjamin in Trumpington and she had been surprised, along with her godmother, to hear from Benjamin that his wife was not recovering properly. Sarah had seemed sprightly enough during their visit.

She entered the drawing room, and Sarah fairly jumped from the sofa to greet her. They embraced.

"Why, Sarah, you are quite well! Your cheeks are blooming," cried Kitty, holding Sarah at arm's length and surveying her with pleasure. "But what reports we have been hearing about you!"

"It is the fault of my overly solicitous husband, I am afraid," apologized Sarah in her soft, slow, almost monotone voice. "Benjamin cannot bear to think of me overexerting myself, you know. He is so good!" She sat down on the sofa again next to Lady

Dinwiddie and complacently righted her bonnet, which had become askew during their embrace, then placed her hands lightly on her knees. "But I am in quite a quandary, for Benjamin said he would be here, and he is not. I resolved to follow him when he told me he meant to visit Ridley Hall and show him that I was not so indisposed as he seemed to think! The fact of the matter is that I am, as you say, Kitty, feeling quite well!"

"You do look in spirits!" concurred Lady Dinwiddie, and Kitty had to agree with her. Motherhood was becoming to Sarah. It had brought more colour to her face and animation to her otherwise too stolid features. Her chestnut hair shone vibrantly and bounced in soft ringlets around her face. Benjamin was a villain to treat the sweet creature so shamefully false, thought Kitty, ire mounting in her breast. And where was he now, she wondered, when he had told his wife he would be at Ridley Hall? And why did he wish to keep Sarah recuperating for so long?

"Have you had a thought to spare for Katherine's ball, Sarah?" asked Lady Dinwiddie, patting Sarah's hand. "We look forward to seeing you there, don't we, Katherine?"

Before Kitty could add her eager request for Sarah's attendance, Sarah said, "Oh, I do not think so! Benjamin will perhaps not be vexed at me for going out against his wishes if he sees I have come to no harm, but he would not countenance a ball. He has already said that the dancing would fag me to death, and ever since I mentioned it to him yesterday he has been even more insistent that I rest. But I cannot lounge forever on my chaise, you know, and be forever in my dressing gown. I am bored to tears."

If Sarah, usually so easy to please and inclined to greatly enjoy mundane domestic routines, was bored, Kitty knew she would have gone mad by now under such confinement. This was too bad of Benjamin! He probably thought that Sarah's presence at the ball would encumber him and thwart some nefarious deed he had in mind. Kitty could only hope that he did not mean to subject her to further insults, because she would be sorely tempted to shoot him, after all! Regardless of her husband, she determined that Sarah would attend the ball. Surely now that they'd seen her in full flourishing health, he could not deny her an evening of dancing, or even Lady Dinwiddie would begin to suspect his motives.

"But, Sarah," she began, "Benjamin could not wish for you to languish away...." Hiller was at the door, coughing discreetly to make his appearance and a wish for their attention known. Everyone turned and he announced the arrival of Mr. Benjamin Whitchurch. Benjamin seemed harried and hot and, removing his beaver hat from his head, tipped it slightly and made a bow which was meant to encompass them all.

"Kitty, Lady Dinwiddie. How d'you do?" Then he turned accusing eyes to his wife. "And so, Sarah, I find you here! I was surprised, to say the least, when I returned to the house to find you had gone out expressly against my wishes!''

"But, Benjamin, I thought you would be here. You said you would be here, did you not?'' Sarah innocently expostulated.

Benjamin seemed momentarily put off guard. "Well...well, so I did. But I found I had a tenant to visit, instead. But that still does not excuse your wandering about alone and in this heat! You are not strong enough yet, my darling,'' he continued in a softened tone.

"But I am! I am, indeed, Benjamin! I came out especially to show you that I am well enough to go about. You must be convinced now, my dear, that I can go about. I do not feel the heat, I assure you.''

"Yes, cousin,'' Kitty added with gleaming eyes that dared him to refute her. "You must now admit that Sarah is well enough to go about amongst her neighbours and friends, all of whom wish her well. And to attend the ball, too. Don't you agree, Lady Dinwiddie, that Sarah is wondrously healthy-looking and strong?''

"You must allow me to be the best judge, ladies, as to my wife's well-being.''

"I do not profess to be a physician, Mr. Whitchurch,'' began Lady Dinwiddie, slightly confused, "but Sarah appears very well to me.''

"But appearances do sometimes belie the truth, my lady,'' Benjamin insisted, pulling Sarah to her feet with a purposeful hand on her elbow.

"Ah," cried Kitty, with sudden inspiration, and gently pulling Sarah down again to her seat on the sofa, "you are no physician, indeed, Godmama. But how fortunate that we have a physician in the house at this very moment. Dr. Rutherford has come to pay his daily call on Sir William. I am sure he would not object to looking at Sarah and giving us his opinion!"

"But I object, cousin," hissed Benjamin between teeth forced into a smile and pulling Sarah to her feet again. "Sarah only needs the loving care of her husband."

"But I do not wish to excite undue attention in anyone," quavered Sarah, looking from one obstinate face to the other. "I am quite well!"

"Then you would not mind if Dr. Rutherford looked at you, Sarah," commanded Kitty, tugging at her skirt and thus throwing her off balance so that she fell with a plop to the sofa again, "if only to put your husband's mind at ease. It must be very painful for him to be always worrying about your welfare, when indeed there may be no need!"

"Taking care of my wife is no hardship for me, I assure you," Benjamin persisted, his face a fierce, glowing mask of suppressed anger. "Dr. Rutherford is not needed here."

"Oh, then she is perfectly well?" inquired Lady Dinwiddie, by now utterly confused. "But you will break her arm, Benjamin, if you do not lessen your grip on it. Her fingers grow blue!"

Benjamin immediately released his wife and endeavored to compose himself by staring at the floor. A muscle twitched convulsively in his jaw, but presently he grew calmer. Turning to Lady Dinwiddie, he said, "I beg your pardon, madam. My concern for my wife makes an animal of me."

"Shall I send for the doctor then and relieve your anxiety, Benjamin?" asked Kitty, all innocent solicitude.

"No, I believe you and Lady Dinwiddie may be correct," he said with an effort. "Perhaps I have overreacted. Sarah may be as well as she claims to be."

"Well, she is the best judge, I am sure!" declared Lady Dinwiddie with satisfaction. "And we may expect to see her for another visit soon?"

"Of course. But now we must go. Come, Sarah." He drew an unresisting Sarah to the door, avoiding looking at Kitty, his mouth a thin, grim line of displeasure.

"Then, cousin," Kitty called out, just as they reached the threshold, "Sarah must be equally fit to attend the ball. Do you not agree?"

Benjamin stopped abruptly but did not look around. He seemed to be struggling again for composure. Sarah looked up at him, her large, brown eyes alight with hope. He sighed resignedly. "Of course, Kitty. I would not dream of keeping Sarah home from the ball." Then, without another word, they left.

"What an odd man your cousin is, Katherine," cried Lady Dinwiddie when the front door had closed behind them. "I had not thought to see such conduct in a gentleman!"

Kitty was surprised to discover that her god-mother, usually so blissfully unaware of anything amiss around her, and with her mind filled continually with matchmaking and fine clothes, had had the penetration to see through Benjamin's feigned anxiety for his wife. She began to hope that she might, upon discussion of the incident, be able to unburden all her secrets concerning Benjamin. It would be a relief to tell her the truth as to why she had left Whitchurch House. But Lady Dinwiddie's next words blighted all hope of such confidence.

"I know he is beside himself with concern for Sarah, but he could have at least bid us a decent good-day! Hmmph! I do not know what is becoming of young people these days when they begin to ignore the commonest of courtesies."

Kitty smiled. Lady Dinwiddie's penetration was as deep and clear as a shallow mud puddle. "Indeed, Godmama. I quite agree with you," she said, taking her godmother's arm in a companionable gesture. Lady Dinwiddie smiled her approbation and they sashayed down the hall quite in harmony with each other.

CHAPTER SEVEN

THE MOON SHONE bright and bold the night of the ball. In fact, the evening was so clear and fair, the breeze so balmy and sweet with fragrance, that Lord Dinwiddie, tweaked no doubt with a youthful whim, decided to light the maze for the entertainment and pleasure of his guests. Candles were dug out of storage by muttering servants, and footmen dispatched to place tall candelabra at each turn in the bushes. The maze was small but intricate. Several servants, hired solely for the ball, were lost for a time, but were eventually recovered by their seniors who had had the honour of being in service at Ridley Hall for years.

Hiller grew instantly more dignified and aloof when Lord Dinwiddie regretfully announced that his services were required in the maze, as seven footmen were still lost in its confines, but he went nonetheless with Mrs. Wells following closely behind, grumbling to herself that she had more than enough to do without baby-coddlin' the hirelings.

But despite his disgruntled servants, Lord Dinwiddie could not regret the sudden inspiration. He remembered with what youthful delight he had run through the maze when it was still a mystery to him. The matrons, the refined and the uncourageous who were afraid of the night air or the inconvenience of losing themselves for an hour or two might stay inside if they wished. There would be enough cautious mothers who would follow their daughters outside to play the part of chaperon, and besides, the maze was just a few yards beyond the French doors opening from the Crystal Room. If guests were to get seriously lost, their cries would be heard eventually, and Lord Dinwiddie himself would tour the maze regularly in search of hapless victims of his caprice.

Kitty had not previously paid much attention to the maze and was unable to enter her hosts' transports.

She did not know why she trembled as she looked out her window and into the lengthening shadows of the late afternoon. She did not fear meeting the gentry who would gather in the rooms below. She would greet them and take each hand with perfect calmness and unconcern. But she sensed that tonight would somehow determine her future, and that thought frightened her.

It was impossible to say if Sir William was close to a declaration of undying love. When he was not with Miss Bidwell, bemoaning and at the same time boasting of the delicate nature of his constitution, he was at her side offering extravagant compliments to her beauty. But he had never mentioned marriage.

Kitty was satisfied that her appearance was good—more than good if Lady Dinwiddie's partiality could be disregarded and her ecstatic assurances believed. The innocently seductive white dress was simple in the extreme, subtly skimming her slender figure. The décolletage was lower than she was used to, and her white skin glowed provocatively above the shimmering silk. Tiny pearls beaded the edge of the high-waisted bodice, and gauzy netting for sleeves exposed her softly rounded shoulders to admiration. A fuchsia sash contrasted gracefully with the white of her dress, and the single pink rose in her hair brought out the lustrous ebony with startling clarity.

A family dinner would precede the ball and Kitty left her room at the appropriate time to gather with the others in the drawing room. Her spirits were subdued, for though she knew Sir William had recovered enough to attend the ball, and he had, in fact, requested her hand for the first set of dances, Kitty did not regard the prospect with pleasure. She was tired of playing a part, but she could see no escape. She felt very much like the orangutan Lord Hatherleigh had compared her to that fateful night at the lake—caged, fettered, and with no hope of escape.

The earl had been avoiding her since the abbey outing, and she had not had one private conversation with him. Thus she had had no opportunity to swallow her pride and ask for her release from the wager. And if the opportunity had arisen, she was not convinced that she would have acted upon it. It seemed cowardly to back out of the arrangement, and in her confused emotional state she was not sure which fate would be worse—marrying Sir William or losing her horse! Sometimes she seemed to feel Lord Hatherleigh's gaze on her or to catch his eye across the room, but he would look away immediately. Kitty wondered what lay behind that intent but covert gaze.

Still in this brown study, with her eyes cast down, Kitty left her room and walked slowly along the hall to the stairs. She was jolted into sudden recognition of her surroundings when her eyes fell on a pair of shiny black slippers. Her gaze continued upward, observing with appreciation the shapely calves in white stockings, the formal black, knee breeches stretched tautly over muscled thighs and an immaculate dark coat. The neckcloth was not too elaborate, nor were the points of the brilliant white shirt too high. This could only be Lord Hatherleigh. His noble features were composed as they looked upon Kitty. At least he did not sneer mockingly—but then he did not smile, either. He merely looked at her, his blue-grey eyes steady and intense.

"My Lord! I see we are ready at the same time," she stammered, her eyes reluctantly drawn to his and unable to look away.

"So we are," he murmured. He tried to pull his gaze away from her, but then began to appraise her in the same leisurely fashion as she had studied him.

Kitty grew self-conscious under the scrutiny but at the same time her senses thrilled. It was as though he were touching her intimately, and she was ashamed to admit to herself the pleasure it gave her.

"You do not look like a young girl going to her first ball, Miss Whitchurch. Oh, you are dressed suitably—wonderfully, in fact. You are lovely as usual, but you are too pale. And you are trembling," he added softly.

"I know," she whispered, finding no ready words to explain her feelings. Everything had become so complicated!

"What? You do not refute my statement and rise haughtily to your own defence?" he queried in a light tone, though his eyes seemed to burn right through her with their unremitting intensity. He spoke in a jesting tone, but Kitty could sense the suppressed energy in his voice and stance.

"I cannot," she finally replied with a slight quaver in her voice. Her thick lashes fell and she stared at his fob, peeking out from the snowy folds of his neckcloth.

He reached forth and lifted her chin with two fingers and claimed her eyes again as though trying to read her thoughts. "Are you regretting your wager, my dear?" he asked.

She felt emotion gather deep in her throat, aching and throbbing to be released. She swallowed hard and nodded.

"Why?" he gently prompted. "Is it because you cannot do it, or because you no longer wish to?"

How could she answer such a question, she wondered, when she did not know the answer herself?

Another door opened down the hall and Kitty started. Lord Hatherleigh's hand fell to his side and he asked, this time with a kind smile, "Will you allow me to escort you downstairs, Miss Whitchurch?"

Kitty smiled her agreement and the earl extended his arm. Hesitantly she slid her hand into the crook of his elbow and they descended the stairs while Lord Hatherleigh began a discussion of the weather. With such a safe subject Kitty was able to calm her tumultuous heart and to greet the others with at least the appearance of normalcy.

"WHERE CAN HE BE?" whispered Lady Dinwiddie to Kitty. "This is later than he has ever been before. If we do not eat soon, we will not have enough time to finish our meal before the guests arrive for the ball."

"He will be down soon, I am sure," soothed Kitty, trying to reassure her godmother. In reality she too was irritated by Sir William's continuing absence. If he had any true regard for her, she thought, he would not cause problems on an evening so important to her, and to the Dinwiddies.

Overhearing the conversation, Miss Bidwell leaned forward to suggest anxiously, "Perhaps he did not consider how long it would take him, in his weakened condition, to dress.''

Kitty could not reply civilly; she merely wondered why Miss Bidwell deemed it necessary to apologize for the wretched man.

''Hmmph!'' was Lady Dinwiddie's only answer, with an exasperated look towards the stairs.

''I will fetch him for you, if you wish,'' said Lord Hatherleigh, as he leaned with nonchalant elegance against the mantelpiece. It seemed to be a favourite place for him to stand, Kitty mused. She would remember him standing thus, long after he and Agatha had departed.

''I would not presume,'' Lady Dinwiddie cried fretfully. ''It would insult him and I fear Sir William has had enough to try him during this visit. Oh, here is his valet coming down the stairs! What can have happened now?''

''Begging your pardon, my lady,'' the valet addressed Lady Dinwiddie. ''Sir William has requested an audience with Miss Bidwell. He has asked me to fetch her for him immediately.'' The valet did not hint, by any change in facial expression, the reason for Sir William's odd request.

''I will go, of course,'' cried Miss Bidwell, jumping up at the first mention of her name. ''I hope he may not have had a relapse!''

''Indeed, I hope he may not!'' exclaimed Lady Dinwiddie. ''For his own sake, to be sure, but also because . . . well, because he has bespoken the first dance with Katherine. And Katherine must begin the ball. Who will stand up with her if he does not?''

"Kitty will have no trouble finding a partner for the first dance, my dear," interposed Lord Dinwiddie. "And we cannot at this point be sure that such substitution will be necessary. Calm yourself, I pray."

"But everyone will think that she has already secured a partner for the first dance. It is the usual thing, you know. All the beaux in the neighbourhood will have secured a favourite for the first dance and there will be nobody left for Katherine!" She rose agitatedly and began to pace the floor, insensible to Lord Dinwiddie's gentle urging that she sit down and wait.

Presently Miss Bidwell descended the stairs. She walked into their midst, with every pair of curious eyes fixed on her and blushed as she felt their interest. "Sir William has the chicken pox!" she announced in her quiet, serious way. "He has only a spot or two that can be discerned on his face, but—" and here she blushed more deeply "—William, er, Sir William has admitted to me that there are other spots of the same appearance elsewhere."

"Oh, no, whatever is to be done? Arthur! Arthur!" Lady Dinwiddie collapsed into a chair, her head lolling in a tragical pose against the cushion. "I shall swoon! I declare I shall swoon! If the guests know that Sir William is down with the chicken pox, they will leave!"

"There, there, dearest," Lord Dinwiddie soothed his wife. "Do not take on so. The guests need not know the exact nature of Sir William's indisposition. He has been sick with a cold for several days and that will be explanation enough for his absence. There is no need for alarm in any event, for no one will come near him and there will not be the least danger for our guests."

Lord Dinwiddie had managed to calm his distraught wife with his sound and reasonable reassurances, but just as she began to breathe more easily, she sat up quite straight and said, "But what about Katherine? Who will lead Katherine to the floor for the first set?"

Cedric Cranfield seemed uncomfortably aware that the task should fall to him. Everyone present either darted a glance or stared outright at him. He cleared his throat and said, "I perceive that you all expect me to apply for the honour of Miss Whitchurch's company for the first dance, but I must beg pardon and decline, for I have already asked Patience Howard for the honour and can hardly retract my invitation without appearing abominably rude."

"You have asked Patience Howard for the first dance?" exclaimed Agatha, until then a mute observer of the ongoing drama. "Why, I did not know you had even seen her since the night she was here several days ago."

"I have, er, seen her several times since then" was Mr. Cranfield's surprising disclosure. "At the parsonage, and once or twice in town."

This announcement flabbergasted everyone in the room. Could the straitlaced Mr. Cranfield have found a kindred spirit in the sober Miss Howard? This happy news might have recovered Lady Dinwiddie completely but for the fact that Kitty still needed a dancing partner.

"Lord Dinwiddie must open the ball with the gel. It is the only thing to be done," put in Lady Cranfield, impatient for her dinner and displeased at the continued delay of her companions. "Or Lord Dinwiddie may get her a partner after the other guests arrive. I daresay some young man will not have secured a partner for the first dance."

"Oh, that is a shabby way to proceed! I cannot do it, sister," cried Lady Dinwiddie. "And what if after all Lord Dinwiddie's exertions all he should be able to dig up at the last minute is Tom Allen, or—"

"Godmama!" admonished Kitty, beginning to feel considerably embarrassed at the fuss being made over what seemed a trivial matter to her. "Tom Allen is a perfectly respectable young man."

"But consider, love, he is a head shorter than you," argued Lady Dinwiddie.

"Then I am sure Lord Dinwiddie will do best of all," Kitty suggested with a mischievous smile, "for he is at least a head taller than I!"

"I will dance with Kitty," said Lord Hatherleigh in a decisive tone as if settling the matter once and for all. "I'm sure Agatha would not object to standing up with her uncle for the first dance. This is Kitty's coming-out ball, after all." Then, as if remembering his duty, he turned to Agatha and asked, "You do not mind, Agatha?"

Agatha was completely devoid of meanness, and gentle and kind by nature. Besides, she seemed to be still reeling under the shock of Mr. Cranfield's admission of an understanding with Patience Howard. "Oh, do please dance with Kitty. I should not mind!"

"My Lord, you have hit upon just the thing," cried Lady Dinwiddie. "I am vastly indebted to you!"

"There is no need for thanks, Lady Dinwiddie," Lord Hatherleigh interrupted with a smile of perfect politeness. "It is no hardship."

Kitty did not know how to feel. She had not anticipated with special pleasure opening the ball with Sir William, and naturally dancing her first dance with her host was not what she had expected. But the earl's offer had set her heart to hammering and her blood to racing through her veins. She stared at Lord Hatherleigh and wondered what had prompted his chivalry. But his lordship did not look at her.

The room became busy as Lady Dinwiddie began to rearrange who should take whom into dinner. As the earl settled Agatha's shawl about her shoulders, he looked up and met Kitty's gaze. She had supposed that Lord Hatherleigh would have done as much for anyone when he offered to begin the ball with her, but as his eyes rested on her now, the expression in them made her feel that the gesture was special, special for her. The idea was disconcerting. She tore her eyes away and took Mr. Cranfield's arm as they proceeded into the dining room.

Dinner was hurried, but Kitty had no appetite to speak of, anyway. When the guests began to arrive and all sallied forth into the Crystal Room, her heart began to beat more quickly than ever. It was beautiful!

The oblong room glowed with candlelight from the three large crystal chandeliers that hung from the vaulted and gilded ceiling. French doors opened to the verdant grounds, and rich damask draperies framed the moon-bathed panes. The orchestra was ensconced above them in a balcony that stretched the width of one end of the ballroom. As they tuned their instruments, the notes—quivering, teasing and bell-like—hung in the air and then floated downward, increasing Kitty's feeling of enchantment.

"Lord Dinwiddie has inclined his head and raised his brows three or four times in your direction, Miss Whitchurch, but you pay him no mind" came a deep, melodious voice from just behind her. Kitty felt his warm breath on her neck as the earl leaned down to address her. "The violinists are poised to begin, and the accomplished young woman on the pianoforte holds her hands suspended above the instrument. We are wanted to begin the ball. Shall we?''

The earl moved in front of her, bowed and reached forth a hand. Kitty placed her hand in his and, taking a deep breath, walked gracefully to the top of the room. She watched with eager delight as the set of dancers formed in an elegant line beside them.

Kitty had not thought a ball could be so glorious. The honour the Dinwiddies were paying her suddenly filled her with warmth and gratitude, and she sought for them in the groups of fashionably dressed people lining the room. At last she found their dear faces, glowing with pride, and she smiled at them with a depth of feeling that surprised her. The music began.

''Ah, if not for my dear, deserving Agatha, I should quite sigh with the thought of those two making a match of it,'' whispered Lady Dinwiddie to her husband. ''What a picture they present! Both so tall and slender, with their striking dark hair and regal bearings. But of course Agatha complements him, too. Her fairness and dainty figure makes him appear more virile and broad of shoulder than ever. And she looks like a porcelain doll next to him.''

''But, my dear, how people look together cannot be a basis for marriage, you know,'' observed Lord Dinwiddie as he too complacently viewed the couple. ''Temperaments, likes and dislikes, backgrounds, intellectual pursuits...all this must be taken into account, you know, to ensure happiness in marriage.''

''Arthur, you do not mean to say that *we* do not look well together, do you?'' asked Lady Dinwiddie in some distress. ''And are happily wed, are we not? You cannot mean to tell me that you married me for my temperament or my intellect? Please say you did not!''

''Well, I will not, then,'' he said with a chuckle, casting her an affectionate look. ''Your beauty infatuated me from the beginning, and—do not eat me if I say so!—your sweet disposition was an inducement, as well.''

''As long as you do not base our happiness on the expectation of intellectual pursuits, I must be satisfied, I suppose. Though you could have said you admired the way I dressed,'' she added mischievously.

''I could not possibly be so unwise as to base our happiness, my dear, on the vain pursuit of intellectual gratification or bookish enthusiasm on the part of my life's companion....''

''Oh, do, my lord, stop humbugging me! You know I do not understand a word you're saying! In plain English, what do you mean?'' cried Lady Dinwiddie.

''Just this, my dear,'' he began, sketching her a gallant bow, ''You look lovely tonight and at all times dress beautifully.''

"Oh, Arthur, how you do go on!" Lady Dinwiddie demurely tapped her husband's arm with the dainty fan she held, finally satisfied with what he had to say. "Now you had best get Agatha for the dance, for the set is almost made up. Go along now!"

"Much as I would like to accommodate you, I cannot. Agatha does not wish to dance the first dance."

"Oh, she isn't upset over the earl's standing up with Katherine, is she? The foolish girl, I must talk with her."

"No, that does not bother Agatha, but I own I do think she is upset," stated Lord Dinwiddie, though he did not appear in the least concerned.

"But pray, why?" enquired Lady Dinwiddie, evidently completely puzzled.

"Time will tell," observed Lord Dinwiddie, smiling enigmatically and walking away to avoid any further questions from his wife.

KITTY WAS TONGUE-TIED. It was an unusual condition for her, and the consciousness of this fact made her more uncomfortable then ever. As the movements of the dance separated her from the earl she racked her brain for a witty or even a commonplace remark, but when the dance brought them together, the touch of his hand on her waist or the brush of his shoulder against hers drove all coherent thought away. He talked and she must have replied, but she was unable at the end of the dance to repeat to herself even one sentence of their conversation.

One thought had occurred to her during the dance, however, and now it stayed obstinately in the forefront of her mind, even though the set had finished. She had been proud and happy to stand up with the earl, even if it were only for a single dance. She imagined it would be a pleasant feeling to repeat. How lucky Agatha was to be able to contemplate such delight throughout her marriage. And she—what was to become of her? She had not felt any pleasure at the thought of opening the ball with Sir William. She couldn't even enjoy dancing with him. How could she consider marrying him?

When Cedric Cranfield claimed her for the next set Kitty was distracted during the first steps, but was jolted out of her own musings by an astonishing remark of her partner's.

"You are severe with me, Miss Whitchurch," said Mr. Cranfield with a bitterly twisted smile. "You think me inconstant and have chosen to be silent as a reprimand."

"Whatever do you mean, Mr. Cranfield?" asked Kitty, her surprise reflected in her face.

"You can't have forgotten my shameful confessions the night of the dinner party with the Howards, can you?" he rejoined, equally surprised. "I have suffered greatly from the knowledge that I ought not to have revealed my affection for Agatha to you. But after a time I grew more comfortable because you did not betray me to anyone, though I could never absolve myself entirely from guilt. It is…*was* wrong of me to cherish such feelings for one who is betrothed to another."

"That is gallant of you, to be sure," said Kitty with feeling, prompted by some reason unclear to herself to sympathize completely with him. "But sometimes people are so beset by their emotions that they cannot overcome them."

"Do you think so? I've always thought it wrong to covet someone belonging to another."

"But she is not married to him yet, you know," insisted Kitty, warming to her subject. "And how can you think that I should accuse you of being inconstant to Agatha while simultaneously believing that you should not be in love with her in the first place? You are making yourself miserable, Mr. Cranfield, with guilt and unrequited love. You must choose which one you would rather endure. I think it vastly unfair for you to be suffering both afflictions together and benefitting not at all from this whole bumblebroth."

"What are you saying, Miss Whitchurch?" Mr. Cranfield was having difficulty following the steps of the dance. His interest in her words clearly occupied his thoughts to the exclusion of all else.

"Just this, Mr. Cranfield," she answered seriously. "If you are determined to suffer from unrequited love, do so and do not feel guilty about turning to someone else to serve as balm to your wounded heart, or..."

"Or?" he questioned, emotion transforming his grave expression to one of eager youthfulness.

"Or do something to feel guilty about! Try to win Agatha away from Lord Hatherleigh!"

"That is ridiculous...isn't it?" He looked anxious and yet hopeful.

Kitty wondered if she were doing the right thing. But she felt driven to continue, for she had an overwhelming conviction that Agatha did not belong with the earl, nor he with her. Neither would be happy in such a match. And she felt the strength of Mr. Cranfield's ardour for Agatha. That would surely more than compensate for the luxuries of life she would forgo by not marrying the earl.

"I do not think it ridiculous at all," stated Kitty firmly, her confidence building at Mr. Cranfield's encouraging response.

"I mean," he began cautiously, "do you think that there is any hope? Do you think I might dare to win her from someone like the earl? She could not possibly prefer me to him, could she?"

"Think about it, Mr. Cranfield. Think about all your daily doings and every conversation you have had with Agatha. Consider her look, her manner when she is around you, then compare them with her look and manner when she is with the earl. Think, Mr. Cranfield, but do not think long! If you are not convinced then that there is hope for you with Agatha, then by all means pursue Miss Howard and feel no guilt about it.''

"Ah, yes, Miss Howard," Mr. Cranfield muttered reflectively. He looked down the set and Kitty followed his gaze. Miss Patience Howard was dancing with her cousin, Benjamin. She was looking livelier than Kitty had ever seen her look before. Benjamin was undoubtedly flirting with her and she was too innocent to imagine his remarks were more than playfulness. But perhaps her vivacity was just a carryover from her previous dance with Mr. Cranfield.

"Mr. Cranfield, you must think of Patience, too. If you have been calling on her she must infer, as does everyone, that you are interested in obtaining her good opinion. You had best take care or you will indeed have something to feel guilty about.''

"Yes," agreed Mr. Cranfield soberly, "I understand you completely, and I must tell you that I began to see her with the best of intentions, that of further acquainting myself with her. When the earl began to treat Agatha with greater consideration I thought it behooved me to fix my thoughts elsewhere. Though I had always imagined that I would appreciate seeing Agatha treated more kindly by her fiancé, I found I was wrong. It was only a different kind of torture for me! I had to get her out of my mind completely, so I tried to occupy and amuse myself with someone else. Miss Howard is a charming young woman with a most refined mind and a nature remarkably suited to a clergyman's life, but she is not..."

"She is not what, Mr. Cranfield?" prompted Kitty.

"She is not Agatha," he concluded with a sigh.

"Well, if your tendre for Agatha is as serious as all that," Kitty gently teased him, "you had best find out somehow, and very soon, if there is any hope for you. I advise you at least to discover whether her feelings for you are completely brotherly. You may find that they are not, and then the rest is up to you."

Mr. Cranfield seemed much struck by this idea. Indeed he was ready to instantly drag Agatha away from her present dancing partner, the earl himself.

Kitty reminded him that it would occasion much talk if he left her stranded on the dance floor, and still more if he accosted Agatha in the manner of a savage claiming his mate.

Seeing the sense of this, Mr. Cranfield contained his enthusiasm, though with much effort, until the end of the set. As he hurried off Kitty felt a moment's doubt. She hoped she had not sent him on a fool's errand that would hurt and humiliate him. But somehow she did not think so.

As Kitty watched Mr. Cranfield head directly for his beloved, she also saw Benjamin approaching her. Sarah had been dancing with one of the Howard boys—Kitty could not tell which—and now seemed to be looking about the room for her husband. Kitty determined that she would not be the one keeping

Sarah's husband away from her and so, turning sharply, walked quickly away. Glancing over her shoulder, Kitty could see by the expression on Benjamin's face that he knew the cut was intentional and was offended. How could he have the effrontery to take offence at her actions? Did he imagine she was obliged to be civil to someone who had attempted her seduction?

A wave of nausea threatened to overcome her when she thought about that last night at Whitchurch House. The heat of the room and the excitement of the ball did not mix well with such unpleasant memories, she decided. She looked longingly towards the French doors that opened to the grounds. Despite the fact that it was insufferably hot inside, the prevailing notion that cool, refreshing air on delicate, heated bodies was unhealthy mandated that the doors be kept closed. Occasionally a young man would steal over and open a door, only to be scolded by an elder as thoughtless and the door would be closed again. It was a pity, Kitty thought, because at that moment fresh air was precisely what she needed.

She looked wistfully at the moonlight playing on the glass and turned reluctantly back to face the room. The Dinwiddies would not wish her to desert the floor so soon. It was her ball, after all.

But turning back, Kitty saw that Tom Allen was approaching her, and—was it possible?—both of the young Howards, and even the squire's son, Jason

Quigly! Jason had tried to steal a kiss from her last summer at the county fair, and she had no intention of dancing with him tonight!

She had a distinct memory of those pudgy lips inexpertly pressed against her chin, nose and ear in an effort to find her lips while she struggled to be released. There he was, grinning like an idiot, looking as though he hadn't a thing to be ashamed of!

Kitty could stand it no longer; she tripped quickly and lightly over to the nearest door, opened it and slipped out. Hiding behind a tall bush, Kitty watched as each pursuing gentleman walked out onto the grass and peered into the dark. Seeing her nowhere, they reentered the house, Tom Allen shrugging in bewilderment.

Kitty stood up straight, breathing in the cool night air. The soft glow from the maze beckoned to her, and she had a sudden, overwhelming desire to go inside. She couldn't hear any laughter or squealing coming from the dense shrubbery. It must still have been too early in the evening for the guests to be tempted outside. Or perhaps the protective duennas had not yet been worn down by repeated requests!

Kitty had a need for solitude that could not be denied. She had conquered the intricacies of the maze long ago, but the enchantment of walking through its leafy quietude, lit by the soft moonlight and wavering candlelight was irresistible. All would be new to her on such a night, and the deserted maze offered the peace and isolation she so ardently desired.

Kitty wandered through the maze, dreamily tilting her head to observe the glittering spray of stars against the velvet blackness of the heavens. Soft, sweet-scented air whispered gently against her skin and lifted the curling tendrils of hair away from her face. Almost immediately she abandoned her original intention of unravelling the confusing details of her life and gave herself up to the intoxicating magic of the mellow, moonlit summer's eve.

Moments later Kitty found herself in a corner of the maze that did not seem familiar to her. She decided that the maze did indeed look different at night, perhaps because familiar markings were obscured in the shadows. And perhaps Lord Dinwiddie had had the benches moved around especially for the ball, and this had added to her general confusion about exactly where she was. Had she turned left last or right? And had it been her third or fourth turn?

A breeze gathered momentum as it whiffed around the corner. A candelabrum stood by the bench, and the flames of the tapers flickered, threatening to extinguish themselves completely, but flaring up again when the air stilled. All at once Kitty knew she was not alone.

CHAPTER EIGHT

SPINNING AROUND, Kitty had the misfortune to find herself face-to-face with a scowling, angry Benjamin. "How did you find me here?" she gasped.

Benjamin looked smug. "I am not the simpleton you think me, cousin. You strolled so leisurely through this tangled puzzle of weeds that I found it an easy task to follow you without being detected."

"What do you want?" Kitty did not like to be alone with Benjamin. Even though she knew she was safe so near to the house, his proximity made her skin creep, and she eased away until the back of her knees pressed against the edge of the bench.

"Do you even need to ask? How dare you cut me like that on the dance floor in full sight of all and sundry!" he snarled. "Everyone in the neighbourhood will be talking about it, and I won't have it, Kitty! Do you hear me?"

"Don't be ridiculous, Benjamin. You were several feet away before I turned and left the floor. No one will connect my action with your approach, though you may be assured that I did wish to avoid you from the bottom of my heart! And I must say,

Benjamin, that I cannot feel any great concern over your reputation."

Benjamin gave a short, derisive bark of laughter. "You are awfully high and mighty for someone without a groat to her name! You were disgustingly high in the instep even when you resided in my home as a dependant, but now that the Dinwiddies have dolled you up for everyone to gawk at, you think yourself of even more consequence!"

Kitty was startled by the vehemence of Benjamin's tone, but still more by the lecherous way his eyes raked her figure. He could not be so idiotic as to try to seduce her within easy distance of a house teeming with people! But as she looked closely at him the flickering candlelight highlighted his face with the hazy, unfocused look of inebriation. Inside the house he had not appeared foxed, but then she had kept herself as far removed from him as possible. He hadn't had time to drink himself into that state at the ball, so she could only assume that he had begun drinking elsewhere. If this were so, she could not depend on him to recognize the nearness of the house or his certain disgrace if he should force himself upon her.

"Benjamin, when you first came to Whitchurch House, I tried very hard to be a grateful friend to you and Sarah," she began in a soothing, reasonable tone. "I did not want enmity between us, but you forced me into it by insulting me in the worst possible way. How could you suppose that any respectable young woman would consent to your odious suggestions!"

"Respectable young woman!" he spat out. "Women are good only for two things, to give men pleasure and bear their heirs. Since you cannot bear me an heir, cousin, and you are admirably modelled to give pleasure..."

"I can't believe you are so stupid Benjamin! Think! You cannot seduce me here on Lord Dinwiddie's own grounds and during my own coming-out ball," Kitty snapped back at him, unable to maintain her placating approach. "Why, I have only to scream and everyone will come rushing out! Lord Dinwiddie would kill you if you dared to touch me!"

"Tonight I am a reckless man, Kitty, darling," crooned Benjamin maliciously. "I lost a great deal of money playing cards last night and in the wee hours of this very morning, and I feel desperate. I may be forced to leave the neighbourhood by those who hold my notes, or pitchforked out by duns within the fortnight, so I might as well go out with a bang instead of a whimper. Though you may whimper if you please...."

Kitty's eyes fixed on Benjamin. He seemed to have grown huge in the flickering light—he loomed out of the darkness, a malevolent hulking shape, coming nearer—reaching out for her.... She was more frightened than she'd been that other night. Benjamin was more desperate now and tonight she had no gun. She opened her mouth to scream.

"If you go one step closer to that girl, you filthy, cheating swine, I'll kill you with pleasure."

Over Benjamin's shoulder Kitty saw the tall, straight form of Lord Hatherleigh. Relief flooded her. She knew she was safe now, and at last her trembling knees collapsed and she sank onto the bench.

"What?" Benjamin turned sharply around, swaying drunkenly as he peered into the half light. "I'll be damned if it isn't you, Hatherleigh. Have I interrupted a little rendezvous?" he sneered.

"One more insult to the lady, Whitchurch, and I'll have you lying at my feet." The earl's voice was low and vibrant with suppressed anger.

"Why don't you leave me alone, Hatherleigh . . . always poking your damned nose into my business!"

"Kitty, go back to the house," said the earl sternly, his eyes never leaving Benjamin's face.

"But I want to know what he means. . . ." Kitty had not missed the implication of Benjamin's comment. Their acquaintance was obviously greater than Kitty had supposed.

"Do as I say!"

The earl's tone did not allow for argument. She got up immediately and walked around the corner, but she did not continue further. Pressing herself into the shadows of a thick bush, she waited until the earl supposed she had indeed removed herself from the immediate vicinity.

"You disgust me, Whitchurch. I knew you cheated on your wife as well as at cards, but I did not think you so low as to accost an innocent girl!"

"What right have you to question my actions?" snarled Benjamin.

"You know damned well what right I have! I scorn to widow your young and hapless wife, otherwise I would long ago have demanded satisfaction from you—satisfaction at twenty paces."

"You contend that I cheated, Hatherleigh, but I still deny it!"

Kitty heard a slight scuffling of feet and a kind of choking sound. She could not contain her curiosity and inched forward, peeking around the bush to observe the two men. Lord Hatherleigh had grasped Benjamin by his neckcloth and was lifting him nearly off his feet. Benjamin's white hands pulled ineffectually at Lord Hatherleigh's forearm.

"I am known as an honest man, Whitchurch. I do not suggest you make any contest of my word against yours. I know you to be a cheat. Many others have suspected it. Once I voice my suspicions you will become a social outcast." The earl dropped him and Benjamin fell back, his face, livid, gasping for breath.

"But I am ruined already," Benjamin croaked, one hand supporting him on the bench and the other stroking his neck. "You cannot punish me more than I have already punished myself. I am deep in dun territory, the reckoning is coming, and then there will be an end to it.''

"Enough mewling, Whitchurch! You defend yourself by crying ruin, but you forget I am well informed of all your financial dealings. Do you recall one night at the Duck and Dog Inn? I found you even deeper in your cups than you are tonight. When you'd exhausted your own cache you dared to wager on your wife's expectations. Spending her yearly income at the gaming table wasn't enough for you! No gentleman at the table was dishonourable enough to encourage you, piteously though you whined!''

"Snake!" hissed Benjamin under his breath.

"And since your wife is indeed wealthy enough to settle your more pressing debts, your sniveling is offensive. Perhaps your only difficulty is convincing her to do so.''

"Sarah denies me nothing." Benjamin stood up and seemed to dare the earl to refute him.

"But she may abandon such easy habits if she learns of a certain special friend you keep in that charming cottage near Somerton," the earl coolly suggested. "I am astonished to discover you can afford such a high flyer, and even more astonished that you have the poor taste to house her so near your own family.''

"How do you know about Fanny?" Benjamin enquired faintly, sinking down onto the bench again.

"Your discretion is not superior, Whitchurch. This night's folly is only one example of your lack of common sense and common decency."

Benjamin fell silent. Evidently he could deny nothing Hatherleigh accused him of. Kitty shook her head sadly. She was thankful her father would never know the kind of a man who had stepped into his shoes as master of Whitchurch House.

Realizing that the earl held all the aces, Benjamin tried to excuse himself and to claim extenuating circumstances. "I admit I have behaved badly towards my cousin, Hatherleigh, but...well, you do not know her as I do! Her forwardness is beyond anything! She has bewitched and encouraged me...."

"If you continue to talk in that manner, Whitchurch, I will knock your head off your shoulders. Kitty has never encouraged you."

"Well, even if she has not," Benjamin exploded angrily, "I was only going to kiss her, perhaps humble that abominable pride of hers!"

"I warn you again, you cowardly snake," the earl ground out, "not to say another word against the lady! And let me further assure you that you will find me a most formidable enemy if you dare accost her or insult her in any way. Do you understand me, Whitchurch?"

Benjamin's mouth pressed tightly together. Kitty listened with glee. She knew her cousin must be longing to make an angry retort, but was too afraid of the earl to speak.

"Well, do you?" thundered Lord Hatherleigh, really raising his voice for the first time.

Benjamin nodded curtly, his mouth working quickly, heavy breaths flaring his aquiline nose.

"And I mean the same conditions for your wife," the earl added authoritatively. "She is an innocent and does not deserve such a wastrel as you. Remember, I have it in my power to destroy you socially and ruin your domestic tranquility, as well. Now be off with you, for I cannot bear the sight of you any longer."

Kitty returned to the shadows of her bush and waited until Benjamin, his head bowed, had stumbled haltingly by. When, after a moment's complete silence, the earl did not follow, she ventured out of hiding and peered around the bush again. The earl stood in the same spot as before, but he, too, had bowed his head and was rubbing the back of his neck as if trying to ease some lingering tension.

Kitty's fingers ached to do it for him. Her heart reached out with tender sympathy and deepest gratitude for the service he had rendered her. Maybe Benjamin had only meant to kiss her, but in his drunken state he could have created an ugly scene.

"Who's there?" The earl swung abruptly around. His eyes widened when he saw Kitty. He said nothing, and long moments passed while she attempted to find her voice. Her lips moved slightly; she desired more than anything to express her thanks but the words would not come. Finally, seeking desperately to communicate with him, she extended her right hand, the fingers white and slender in the moonlight.

His eyes dropped to her outstretched hand and followed the lines of her arm to the hollow of her throat, then upwards to her lips, now straining to form a smile.

Somehow she must thank him! It was an urgent need, an overwhelming compulsion! "My Lord, I cannot find the words..." Her voice was a mere whisper on the wind.

"Words are not necessary, Kitty," the earl murmured, his voice husky and low. Then to Kitty's pleasure and consternation, he caught her hand in his and pressed it against his chest. Kitty could feel the steady throb of his heart beneath her quivering fingertips and she gasped.

"I thought to rescue you from your odious cousin, but who will deliver you from me?" he continued in the same low, hypnotizing voice. He lifted her hand to his lips and kissed the palm, pink and warm from the pressure of his chest. "Who, Kitty?" he persisted, kissing one finger and then another. "Who, my darling Kitty?"

Kitty felt she must sink with the sensation of his lips against her skin. She moaned softly and the earl gasped sharply at the sensuous sound. He released her hand and pulled her to him. His eyes restlessly devoured every feature of her face, and finally settled with unmistakable purpose on her lips.

She longed for the feel of his warm, firm mouth against hers again. She'd never forgotten that night on the road, and tonight their kiss would feel even more wonderful, because she loved him. She pressed against the strong, lean length of his body, revelling in the blissful torture.

"Ahem!"

"Lord Dinwiddie!"

"Sir!"

Kitty and Lord Hatherleigh leapt away from each other with the speed of guilt prompted by the humility of exposure. The earl looked as if he'd awakened from a pleasant dream and suddenly realized the folly of thinking it could be real. Kitty burned with disappointment mixed with shame.

What would the Dinwiddies think of her now? They had brought her into their home and treated her like a daughter, and what had she done to repay them? She had betrayed, indeed had wanted to betray, Agatha's friendship and their confidence by enticing Lord Hatherleigh! And what must the earl think of her? How shameful, disloyal and brazen she must appear to him!

"I know how this must appear, Lord Dinwiddie," began the earl in a strained voice. "And I will not try to mollify you with lies. It is entirely my own fault. Kitty, er, Miss Whitchurch is beyond reproach. Finding her in the moonlight like this, and looking so lovely, I lost my head...."

"Spare me your honourable excuses, Lord Hatherleigh," Lord Dinwiddie interrupted in an ironic voice laced with a touch of amusement. "We shall discuss this later."

Daunted by this speech, Kitty and the earl gazed at him. How could Lord Dinwiddie view such an episode so composedly?

"But, sir," began the earl, his thick, dark brows pulling together forbiddingly.

"I insist that we delay the confessions for later, young man," Lord Dinwiddie persisted, taking on a more serious demeanour as though he knew they expected it of him. "There is still a ball to be played out you know. A Cheltenham tragedy will only complicate the proceedings and render your godmother, Kitty, apoplectic. She has been looking for you for the past ten minutes as it is, and you must present her with a believable explanation."

"Oh, I understand, sir," Kitty agreed in a small voice. "I will return instantly and tell her that I unfortunately lost myself in the shrubbery. One of my whims, you know. And that, at least, is the truth," she added humbly.

"I will escort Kitty back to the house, Hatherleigh. You may follow in a few minutes."

The younger peer of the realm acknowledged Lord Dinwiddie's authority with a curt nod. The look he gave Kitty as she walked away was deeply pained and apologetic. But Kitty felt there was nothing to forgive. She was as much at fault as he was.

But she couldn't help a tiny, lingering regret. If only Lord Dinwiddie had arrived just a minute later! Just one minute and their lips would have met. Kitty sighed. Whatever the consequences, she knew she would never forget the magic spell of that enchanted evening.

SEVERAL HOURS LATER as she lay in her bed, Kitty knew that sleep would elude her. Not even the dawn breaking over the distant hills surrounding Lord Dinwiddie's estate would bring her repose. She had fixed a pleasant smile on her face for the duration of the ball. Even the highest stickler present, a turbaned, hook-nosed dowager with a pedigree unequalled in the nearby countryside, had declared her a charming, well brought up chit. Others who had known Kitty as a child acknowledged that she'd outgrown her hoydenish ways and would be eagerly sought after in the London season, even without a fortune to match her considerable beauty.

Kitty stood it all with stoic fortitude. The consciousness of what she owed the Dinwiddies had been foremost in her thoughts. Her heart ached with an empty desolation whenever she thought of the earl, but these pains were tempered by the condemnation she showered on her own head for her shameless behaviour. She wished desperately that she did not love him. The condition had been creeping up on her from the moment they'd met, but she had been too naive to recognize the symptoms.

She had taken the physical and mental excitement he stimulated in her as something quite different. The sparring in words, the quick irritations had all been due to her stubborn denial of her true feelings. Who had ever said that opposites attracted?

Nathan Alexander was more herself than she was, their temperaments exactly complemented each other. Agatha only tolerated his high-handedness and caustic humour; she did not understand him in the least. How Kitty would relish long winter nights duelling with the earl in spirited conversation, the two of them secretly in total agreement with each other but loath to admit it. And when conversation waned . . .

Kitty pressed her face into her pillow, letting the slow tears trickle into the cool linen. With the movement of her body Cleopatra stirred against her leg and meowed complainingly. Kitty had not drawn the curtains at her window, and as she looked down at her pet, Cleopatra's luminous green irises reflected the moonlight. She sighed. The guests had all left nearly two hours ago. It must be nearly dawn.

What was that? Kitty did not think she could have mistaken the sound of footfalls on the paved walk below her window. She had left the window open wide hoping the gentle night air would encourage sleep. Jumping from her bed, she reached the window just in time to discern a tall figure vanishing round towards the back of the house. It was too early for the servants to be up, and besides the figure had appeared to be wearing a tall beaver hat in the current fashion of a gentleman. Kitty wondered who it might be.

The breeze molded Kitty's, or rather, her father's, nightshirt to her body as she leaned farther out of the window. There was nothing to be seen and nothing to be heard but the singsong of crickets from the lake and an occasional mournful bellow from a bullfrog. Several moments passed, and though she was not satisfied to leave the mystery thus unsolved, the night air and the interruption of her former melancholy thoughts had done the trick. She was sleepy.

She returned to her bed and quickly lapsed into a state of semiconsciousness. She thought she heard the sound of a horse's hooves carry through the stillness of the night, but she drowsily decided that it was a dream . . . a dream that quickly moved into a vision of herself riding with the earl on his glorious Lightning, her arms wrapped around his waist and her face pressed against his broad back. . . .

"YOU HAD BEST GET UP, MISS. There's goin's on downstairs. They might need you to help."

Kitty buried her face deeper into the soft plumpness of her pillow. She had enjoyed the most delicious dreams throughout the night and she did not want to release her place in such a pleasant kingdom for the harsh realities of real life. "Go away, Leah. I want to sleep."

"Her ladyship is in a fair way t'makin' herself sick, Miss Katherine, and if you feel any gratitude to your godmother you'd best get up and show it."

Kitty blinked and focused on the rose-patterned wallpaper opposite her bed. Memory flooded vividly back. Last night, the earl, the moonlight, Lord Dinwiddie, Agatha...

Oh no! Perhaps Lord Dinwiddie had disclosed the whole of last night's folly to Lady Dinwiddie! What if there had been a confrontation between the earl and Lord Dinwiddie? Perhaps it had been the earl she'd seen leaving the house in the dark of the early morning hours! Had he been compelled to leave?

Kitty instantly jumped out of bed. She must know all as soon as possible. "Leah, make haste! Bring me a gown, any gown! And do not fuss with my hair! I must see what the matter is. Tell me all you know."

But Leah could not reveal much more than she already had. All she knew was that Lord and Lady Dinwiddie were shut up in his study and Lady Dinwiddie had been conveyed to that area of the house leaning weakly against her husband's shoulder. Miss Bidwell was stealing in and out of the room with bottles of lavender water, gently closing the huge oak doors behind her. But when the doors were open Lady Dinwiddie's distress was quite audible to all the servants who had somehow found employment just outside Lord Dinwiddie's study. To cap it all, Leah had passed Lady Cranfield in the hallway on her way to wake Kitty. In the maid's words, her ladyship was "lookin' to spit fire, miss. I never did see her move so fast, or look so furious!"

Kitty could hardly bear to think she might be the source of all this distress. But upon serious deliberation, she felt there must be more to it. She doubted that Lord Dinwiddie had even mentioned her moonlight encounter with the earl to her godmother. He knew better than anyone the excitable disposition of his wife. And no one in his right mind would dare report such information to the mother of the bride-to-be, would he?

Leah released Kitty at last, much later than Kitty had wished. But despite her fidgets and complaints Leah would not dismiss her mistress to the view of others until she was fit to be seen. Kitty swept out of the room in a flutter of fresh muslin, her hair braided at the temples and left to fall freely in the back. Glancing in the oval mirror in the hall outside the study, Kitty realized that Leah must have picked the dress especially. Its deep rose hue did much to brighten her face, grown pale and slightly drawn from lack of sleep and the accumulation of unexpected burdens in the form of hopeless love. She steeled herself for whatever lay beyond the oaken doors. Then she turned the large brass knob and entered the room.

"Oh, how shall we tell him? It pains me horribly to think of it! So in love! So right for each other! They looked so well together, you know!" Lady Dinwiddie sniffed dolefully into a handkerchief.

"Good God, what has happened?" Kitty asked, taking in the scene with incredulous wonder. Lady Dinwiddie lay prostrate on one sofa and Lady Cranfield reclined in the same position on the other. Miss Bidwell was trying to minister to both at once, but it seemed a well-nigh impossible task since each lady appeared to require constant attendance.

"But perhaps he has followed them and means to kill them both! Scorned lovers have been known to act upon their jealous passions in such circumstances!" came Lady Cranfield's muffled wail from beneath the cascading folds of the huge handkerchief pressed against her temples.

"Oh, do not say so, sister! In such cases the jilted lover may only feel honour bound to dispense with the other gentleman! We must be brave! We must not lose hope!" This last utterance was accented by a pitiful sob, leaving Kitty to conclude that in her godmother's estimation the situation was hopeless, indeed.

She looked about the room for Lord Dinwiddie, hoping he would be able to provide her with a sane explanation. She found him leaning into the recess of a windowed alcove, looking out over the grounds with a thoughtful but scarcely frantic expression. Promising Teresa that she would return to help her in a moment and receiving that lady's grateful nod, Kitty left the sisters to their lamentations and walked over to Lord Dinwiddie.

"Good morning, Kitty. You slept late this morning," observed Lord Dinwiddie, casting her an appreciative glance and returning his gaze to the window.

"And missed all the excitement, I gather," she returned, impatient for the news, yet dreading that it might include the information that Lord Hatherleigh had left the premises.

"There will be more excitement, to be sure," Lord Dinwiddie assured her with a grin.

"You are not as distressed as the others, my lord," observed Kitty, her mind racing at all the possible disasters that might have befallen the household. "So perhaps I am silly to be afraid of what you may have to tell me?"

"It is simply this, my dear." Lord Dinwiddie reached over and took one of her cold hands in both of his large, warm ones. "Agatha and Cedric Cranfield have eloped."

"You don't mean it! Can it be possible? Cedric Cranfield actually dared to elope with a girl, and with Agatha at that? And right under the nose of her fiancé?" Kitty pulled away from Lord Dinwiddie and sat down on the nearest chair. Straitlaced, proper Mr. Cranfield, the future rector of Flatford Mill, violently disapproving of the humanity around him at worst, and reserved at best, this same Mr. Cranfield had thrown caution to the winds and flung propriety into the teeth of a very proper society and carried his lady love away to Gretna Green!

Kitty felt a giggle coming on. Never in a million years would she have imagined that her little talk with Cedric could have brought about such a result. Cedric must only have been waiting for that nudge to fulfil his deepest wishes. And Agatha must have realized the depth of her affection for her stepbrother when the possibility of a romance with Patience Howard was pressed upon her. Well, that is that, thought Kitty, feeling a little like Cupid. While surprising, it was hardly a disaster, so what was all this talk about violence, passion and murder?

Kitty stood up and returned to stand near Lord Dinwiddie. "Why does my godmother talk of hoping for the best, my lord? Surely Lord Hatherleigh has taken the news like a reasonable man. I find him a most sensible man, don't you?"

"Well, Kitty," chuckled Lord Dinwiddie, still looking out over the grounds, "as we can see by the happenings of this day, sometimes reason eludes a man inflamed by jealousy."

"But surely you do not think the earl is so very jealous," Kitty blurted out. "I mean," she amended quickly, "of course his pride may be wounded, but as to his affections . . ."

"You may be the better judge of that, I daresay," Lord Dinwiddie suggested with a twinkle in his eye, "but I will withhold my judgement of the affair until I have spoken to the gentleman himself."

"You mean he does not know?" Kitty enquired. "You don't suppose he does know and has gone after them, do you? Is that why you stand at the window, Lord Dinwiddie? You are watching for the earl?''

''I think his lordship has gone on a morning ride to clear the cobwebs from his mind, child,'' Lord Dinwiddie said, ''and I wish to intercept him before he is set upon by the two sadly prostrated ladies lying yonder. They look pallid and weak enough now, but you may be sure that when Hatherleigh walks into the house he will be met with enough weeping and wailing to overset any man. I must make sure he has time to think and prepare a proper response.''

''A proper response...? I'm afraid I don't understand you, sir,'' said Kitty. ''What do you—''

''Ah, there he is! Do not betray me to the others, Kitty. They are happily occupied just now in their mutual grief. I must talk to Hatherleigh alone.''

Kitty watched as Lord Dinwiddie leaned over his wife and patted her hand. Then after exchanging a few low, soothing words with her, he left the room. She looked out the window just as the earl reached the gravelled drive at the side of the house. He slid out of the saddle even before his spirited mount had changed from its lively trot to a more sedate speed. His booted feet hit the ground with athletic precision and he reined in his horse with an expertise that Kitty could not help but thoroughly admire. She saw Lord Dinwiddie join him at the edge of the lawn and turn to walk with him to the stables.

Remembering her promise to Teresa, Kitty joined her in tending her distraught godmother and Lady Cranfield. It was an exhausting exercise in compassion, however, even though she loved her godmother dearly. That lady's constant speculations on the dire consequences of Cranfield and Agatha's folly were becoming increasingly tiresome. And she could not care, either, to hear interminable repetitions of how very much dear Nathan had loved Agatha and how devastated he must be at the elopement.

Naturally Kitty could not suppress a hope that the earl would bear with fortitude the news that his fiancée had been spirited away by another man. Her happiness depended on believing his lordship's feelings would be quite other than devastation. But then came a dampening thought.

Why should she believe she and the earl had a future together? Perhaps it was just her own wishful thinking. He was free now, that was true enough. But had his attentions to her been just an amusing fancy to pass the time while he rusticated in the country with Agatha's relatives? Had she imagined more emotional involvement on the earl's part than truly existed? And even if the earl did care for her, she was portionless, and worse yet, closely related to a man he loathed—her cousin, Benjamin.

As she remembered that conversation between Benjamin and Lord Hatherleigh last night in the maze, she also recalled the wager she'd so foolishly entered into with the earl. He must think gambling a family failing, thought Kitty ruefully as she dabbed additional lavender water on her godmother's already soaked handkerchief. At least she did not cheat, like Benjamin. But if she sought to be released from the wager, wouldn't the earl think her as dishonourable as her cousin?

Obviously Lord Hatherleigh maintained the highest standards in such matters. Kitty sighed. It was too confusing. Her brain was muddled and her heart heavy. There was nothing she could do until the earl expressed his true feelings, so she decided she must try to wait patiently and see what he would do.

This was easier said than done, though, and the next hour wore sadly on Kitty's nerves. Lady Dinwiddie would not be comforted and Lord Dinwiddie did not come. When Kitty began to lose hope completely, Lord Dinwiddie finally reappeared, but he was alone.

"What is it, Arthur? You know something, don't you? Has Nathan killed Cedric? Tell me immediately! I must be strong!"

Lady Dinwiddie had bolted upright when her husband entered the room, disregarding totally the burnt feathers Kitty had been waving in front of her nose. Feathers flew, but no one regarded the mess. Everyone's attention was riveted on Lord Dinwiddie.

"Calm yourselves, ladies. Until moments ago Lord Hatherleigh was completely unaware that Mr. Cranfield had absconded with his bride-to-be."

"But how did he take the news?" Lady Cranfield demanded as she, too, struggled to a sitting position.

"With strong emotions."

"Of course he would be utterly overcome," agreed Lady Cranfield with a ponderous sigh. "And it pains me so to see such an eligible, delightful man thus excluded from becoming a part of our family!"

Kitty thought that Lady Cranfield felt more grief at parting with the earl's title and fortune than with his actual self. Agatha was exchanging a high position in the ton for the relative obscurity of a country parson's wife. But Kitty did not think that Lady Cranfield had ever seriously considered her daughter's feelings about marriage to the earl. Her ladyship had manoeuvred her daughter into the engagement, dazzled by the prospect of such a brilliant match. But Kitty could not entirely condemn Lady Cranfield. The polite world viewed marriage in this mercenary light, and hadn't she been guilty of a similar short-sighted view in her own pursuit of Sir William?

But even as she came to these conclusions, Kitty felt increasing unease at Lord Dinwiddie's choice of words. He had said that the earl had reacted to the news of Agatha's elopement with strong emotions. Just exactly what had the earl felt? Her host had seemed to imply that Lord Hatherleigh was heartbroken. At least that was how the other women had chosen to view his report.

"Where is the earl now?" Kitty asked.

"He has ridden into Barley. He means to take a room at the Black Swan for the evening. He has commissioned me to send his valet and a few clothes and of course to convey his regrets to you, ladies."

"He means to avoid us altogether?" cried Lady Dinwiddie, supposing they had made a mortal enemy of the earl.

"No, no, my dear. He will return to Ridley when he is in better control of himself. He does not hold us accountable for Agatha's actions. He will return and bid us a civilized goodbye, but for a time he feels the need to be alone with his thoughts."

"The poor man," Miss Bidwell clucked sympathetically. "I feel for him exceedingly."

Everyone in the room grew silent then and appeared absorbed in his or her own thoughts.

"But what about Sir William?" After a moment's interval Lord Dinwiddie briskly addressed Miss Bidwell. "Our spotted guest holds some claim to our sympathy, as well. How does he go on? I know you spent the greater part of last evening seeing to his comfort, Miss Bidwell, and I am sorry that you missed so much of the ball because of it."

"He is doing fairly well," Miss Bidwell eagerly supplied. "But I own I have been uncomfortable at leaving him solely to the ministrations of his valet this morning. Perkins is a very capable person, to be sure, but Sir William has shown a preference for my aid," she shyly admitted.

"And who would not?" Lord Dinwiddie said, chuckling as he patted her lightly on the arm. "Return to him immediately. I will send for my wife's and Lady Cranfield's abigails to attend to them now. There is no point in trying to hide the events of this day from our servants. I can well imagine that the story is halfway to Trumpington by now, anyway, and it will be a juicy tidbit for the *Gazette* by next week. It will be interesting to see how it finally appears in print. Gossips are notorious for changing details as the story is spread."

"Arthur, how can you jest about it?" Lady Dinwiddie wailed. As she continued to reprimand her husband for his obvious lack of proper feeling on the subject, Lady Cranfield actually managed to summon up enough energy to join in. But since Lord Dinwiddie seemed to be withstanding the verbal abuse with utter unconcern, Kitty did not feel her presence was any longer required. She followed Miss Bidwell from the room, with every intention of retiring to her bedchamber. She wished to brood over that morning's drama and calculate just how soon they might expect to see the earl on the morrow.

CHAPTER NINE

"Miss Whitchurch?"

"Yes?" Kitty replied automatically as she ascended the stairs with Miss Bidwell, but her mind was far away.

"I did not want to bring it up in the study—it did not seem appropriate!"

"What is it, Miss Bidwell?" asked Kitty, her interest piqued by Teresa's air of hesitancy. "I daresay nothing you could say at this point would alarm or surprise me," she added with a smile.

"Oh, it is not alarming, or in any way surprising, I suppose. It is only that Sir William has especially requested to see you this morning." Miss Bidwell relayed this message in a rather subdued voice and kept her eyes fixed on the banister rail.

"Well, I certainly was wrong to tell you that nothing you could say would surprise me, Miss Bidwell, because I own I am *very* surprised! Sir William is the unwilling victim of a disease which indiscriminately pocks its victims, and he still wishes me to see him, even in such a state! You know, Miss Bidwell, how fastidious Sir William is about his appearance! Why...?"

"I can only suppose that his desire to see you, and his indifference to his appearance, arise from the attachment I have noticed he has for you," Miss Bidwell replied in the same quiet manner. "Forgive me if I am too familiar, Miss Whitchurch," she blurted out a moment later, finally looking at Kitty. "But is there some sort of an understanding between you and Sir William? I overheard Lady Cranfield and your godmother talking one day and from the conversation could only conclude that a marriage between you is to be expected."

They had reached the landing, and Kitty was feeling very uncomfortable under the earnest, enquiring look leveled at her by Miss Bidwell. Sir William had definitely made a friend out of this gentle creature, thought Kitty, for she seems to take as much interest in his personal life as in his physical well-being. But she hadn't a clue as to what to say to Miss Bidwell. To admit that she'd had a bet with the earl would expose her in a very unflattering light, and would perhaps alienate the girl from her forever. Kitty found that she very much valued Miss Bidwell's good opinion. She decided to avoid a direct response.

"Gentlemen may sometimes appear to be serious when in reality they are only flirting," she said in a light tone. "I once read that it was not entirely proper for a woman to fall in love with a man unless he had clearly represented his own affection for her in the form of a proposal of marriage!" When she first saw it, Kitty had thought this notion extremely stupid, for how could one suppress one's feelings and only unleash them in a torrent of passion when it was deemed the proper moment? But now she wished only to forestall Miss Bidwell. She could not tell her the truth—that she had been leading Sir William on for the contemptible purpose of acquiring a wealthy husband and winning a bet. Furthermore, she now had no intention whatsoever of marrying Sir William, even if her blatant encouragement had unhappily succeeded.

"I have heard it said that men are sometimes misleading in their flirtations," Miss Bidwell agreed, her honest face grave and confused. "But I thought I perceived a willingness on your part, Miss Whitchurch, to accept Sir William's attentions."

Kitty grew pink with shame. What if she had engaged Sir William's affections with her coquettish play-acting? She had not wished to wound anyone, but she had to own her thoughtless behaviour might well have done so. If only she'd known her heart three weeks ago as clearly as she understood it today! But hindsight would not aid her now. She must face Miss Bidwell's uncomfortably direct questioning. Just as she became convinced that she must tell her the truth, Sir William's valet appeared.

Looking accusingly at them, he announced "Sir William is waiting for you, Miss Whitchurch and, if I may say so, he's growing fidgety in the extreme."

Miss Bidwell responded immediately to this plea from the faithful servant, and Kitty was eager to comply with her suggestion that they enter Sir William's parlour without delay.

They found the patient in the sitting room which adjoined his bedchamber. He sat on the chaise longue, dressed in an elegant robe and propped up with several pillows. This was remarkable to Kitty, who had assumed that the hypochondriac in Sir William would dictate exclusive bed rest and constant attendance by a physician. The thought occurred to her that his willingness to forgo such pampering might be a sign of affection for her, and she grew sober.

"Miss Whitchurch! Ah, it is a pleasure to see you again. How can I ever apologize enough for abandoning you last night. But Miss Bidwell assures me that you did not lack for partners and you were the acknowledged belle of the ball. But how could it be otherwise?"

Except for the spots on his face, Kitty thought Sir William looked very well. His cheerful attitude astonished her, however, and she barely managed a polite smile as she sat down opposite him on another couch. Miss Bidwell fussed about, plumping his pillows and measuring some kind of medicinal potion into a glass.

"Sir William, you amaze me!" she ventured to say at last. "I had not thought to see you so hale and hearty! You do not succumb to the inconveniences of the chicken pox at all!"

Sir William laughed, and Kitty stared. "I have been so well nursed by Perkins and Miss Bidwell that

I do not feel the inconveniences, as you so wittily describe the symptoms of this absurd disease. After all, when Miss Bidwell's brothers had the chicken pox they could still summon up enough energy to plague their governess with tadpoles in her wash basin! So I am persuaded I may survive, as well!''

Although Kitty knew Sir William to be optimistic by nature, she could hardly contain her astonishment at his present positive attitude towards the misfortune that had befallen him. At the Kimballs' he had not been so sanguine when first told that he might catch the unsightly disease. Kitty supposed she must give Miss Bidwell the credit for fostering such a welcome change in outlook.

As Sir William prattled on, complimenting her in his flamboyant way, Kitty glanced up at the ministering angel who had wrought this change in Sir William and was arrested by the soft, flushed radiance of Miss Bidwell's expression. She seemed to be thoroughly enjoying her role as benevolent nurse. Kitty felt something like envy creep into her heart. She wished she could have been as unselfish and so happily willing to see to another human being's comfort. But then she had been eager to make her father comfortable when he was ill, barely leaving his side during those last weeks when he could not move from his bed. And if the earl were to fall ill, nothing could prevail upon her to allow anyone but herself to plump his pillows and . . .

Good heavens! Kitty began to suspect that her preoccupation with Lord Hatherleigh had blinded her to every obvious human condition surrounding her! Miss Bidwell must be in love with Sir William! A kind-hearted disposition had undoubtedly prompted her initial solicitude on his behalf, but it had escalated into something akin to complete devotion! What could account for this except a romantic attachment? And this would also explain Miss Bidwell's probing questions concerning her own relationship with Sir William!

But Kitty was not at leisure to pursue the topic further, for Sir William had suddenly taken her hand, declared it to be uncommonly cold and was chafing it between his two warm ones. Kitty recognized the excuse to hold her hand. She had allowed him to do this in the past, and he was astonished when she drew back and looked at Miss Bidwell in obvious alarm.

Kitty had no wish to give Miss Bidwell pain. She could not possibly enjoy watching the person she dearly loved flirting openly with another. Kitty cringed when she thought of all the anguish she must already have inflicted on Teresa's vulnerable heart.

"I'm sure Lady Cranfield must be wishing for me," Miss Bidwell murmured, turning her head away from them and beginning to walk towards the door. Kitty realized that Miss Bidwell and Sir William had interpreted the reclaiming of her hand as mere maidenly modesty. Miss Bidwell must have been supposing that she wished to be alone with Sir William!

Panic constricted her throat and Kitty's croak of "No! Do not go, Miss Bidwell!" surprised the other two with equal force. They stared at her while she attempted to gather her thoughts, but Perkins again most fortuitously rescued Kitty from another uncomfortable situation.

"Lady Cranfield wishes to have a word with you, Miss Bidwell," he announced solemnly.

"Then I will go."

"It is not necessary, Teresa" came Lady Cranfield's authoritative voice as she pushed Perkins out of the way and stationed herself in the doorway. "Perkins here has some ridiculous idea that it is unhealthy to crowd the sick room with too many visitors, but as I did not come to visit I am sure nothing will go amiss if I enter for a moment. You look well enough, Sir William, considering," she added as an afterthought. "But I am only come to tell Teresa that she must pack immediately. We will be off within the next two hours."

"We will be off? To where, madam?" Teresa was clearly distressed by the announcement.

"Home, of course, gel! There's no point in lolly-gagging around here till the earl takes it into his head to return. He may never return, for all we know! And I've no taste to sit around and discuss this tawdry tale day after day. The whole place plunges me into gloom just looking at it. We made a mistake coming here and throwing those two together! But who would have thought any gel in her right mind would even look at Cranfield when the earl was about!"

"You mean to leave me behind?" Sir William asked Lady Cranfield piteously, showing the first signs of distress since Kitty entered the room.

"I do, Sir William" was Lady Cranfield's unsympathetic response. "You will be knocked up for at least two weeks, and I cannot abide staying here that long. You are in good hands. You may send for your coach whenever you are ready, or I am sure Lord Dinwiddie will lend you his vehicle to convey you to town once you are recovered."

"But, but…" faltered Sir William, as he drooped pathetically on his pillows, despair clouding his eyes.

"But what, Sir William?" cried Lady Cranfield impatiently.

"Miss Bidwell has been taking care of me. Can't she stay? I need her to…"

"You have Perkins. Miss Bidwell must be returned to her family. It would be most improper for me to leave her behind when her mother has entrusted me with her care."

"But surely my mother would agree to let me stay here for a while if I write to her and request it," Teresa suggested.

"I do not have time to wait for you to get consent from your mother, Teresa," Lady Cranfield curtly returned.

"But Lady Cranfield, I do *so* want to stay. Cannot you just tell my mother that I will follow you in a week or two? She might send James for me," Miss Bidwell timidly implored.

"The matter is settled," Lady Cranfield snapped. Kitty could tell her ladyship had been shocked out of her usual indolence by her daughter's elopement. Her spirits were irritated to the point of waspishness. But she needn't take it out on Teresa! She was about to place herself in peril by saying so when Sir William spoke again.

"You needn't speak in that tone to Miss Bidwell. She is not the cause of your present dilemma. And she has been nothing but a comfort to me. I insist that you leave her here. She does not want to go and I do not want her to go." Sir William's face had grown livid, but instead of blending in with this new colour, the spots on his face grew even more pronounced.

Kitty was forcefully reminded of a wormy beetroot when she looked at him. Dismissing the unflattering comparison, she could not help but be impressed by his defense of Miss Bidwell.

Lady Cranfield, however, viewed the situation quite differently.

"Sir William, you have absolutely no right to an opinion on the subject. You met Teresa's parents once, and then only briefly. If I were to inform them that she had stayed behind to nurse a gentleman—a bachelor gentleman at that!—with whom they were barely acquainted... Why, anyone might understand their natural hesitation in the matter."

"I've given my parents no cause in the past to question my judgement," Teresa bravely interjected. "And if I choose to stay behind and nurse Sir William..."

"You are such a child, Teresa, in the ways of the world!"

"If you mean to imply, Lady Cranfield," began Sir William, a quiver of indignation in his words, "that I might take advantage of this young girl..." Sir William's indignation at Lady Cranfield's ill-natured implication was so great that he was attempting to stand up. He gripped the chaise and in his weakened state his arms trembled with the exertion.

"Oh! Sit down, William!" cried Miss Bidwell, appalled that he should be working himself into such a frenzy. "It is not wise to excite yourself. There is danger of a fever if you do!"

"But I cannot allow her to order you about in such a way, Teresa!"

"*William*, it is! *Teresa*, you say! Indeed!" Lady Cranfield conveyed her extreme disapproval of these familiarities by raising her nose high in the air and sniffing loudly. "I can see that I have been remiss in allowing you as much freedom as I have, Teresa! Go to your room immediately and supervise the packing of your trunks, if you please!"

"Do not badger the girl!" protested Sir William, beads of sweat forming on his brow.

"I beg of you, Lady Cranfield, I will do exactly as you wish if you will leave the room immediately! You are making Sir William quite ill!"

Lady Cranfield snorted derisively, folded her beefy arms across her ample chest and leveled a smouldering gaze at Sir William. Her ladyship was venting her spleen on the two of them merely because they had come in her way at a bad moment. Had her daughter been there, this seething anger would have been directed at her, but now Sir William and Teresa were the recipients of Lady Cranfield's wrath. Kitty had to admit that the confrontation had produced some interesting results. She looked from Sir William to Lady Cranfield and waited to see what would transpire.

"Now look here, Lady Cranfield," began Sir William. But he was seized by a jab of pain at the temples. He pressed his fingers against the throb and grimaced grotesquely. This was the deciding factor, the turning point of the scene, as it were. Teresa was furious. She turned on her best friend's mother as a tigress might turn on a threat to her cub.

"See what you have done!" she hissed, her gentle face most uncharacteristically hostile. "I insist that you leave now! I will brook no opposition, Lady Cranfield! You have gone too far!"

Lady Cranfield was more than a little surprised to see the heretofore submissive lamb transformed into a worthy adversary. But primed for battle, her lady-ship did not shrink from the fray. "You take an uncommon interest in that gentleman's well-being! I daresay your parents would not view the matter so complacently!"

"Even if my parents were so addled as to suspect scandal here, I think I should not care! I will stay!"

"Teresa!" Sir William's voice was feeble, but still resonant with feeling. He gazed enraptured at his valiant champion and was rewarded by the brilliant glow in her eye as she stood staunchly before Lady Cranfield. Passion and conviction had rendered the plain girl beautiful—especially to Sir William. The extent of Teresa's devotion was suddenly obvious to him and his own true wishes struck him like a bolt of lightning! He could not do without Teresa—not now, not ever! And the only way to bind her to him permanently was through the bonds of matrimony.

"I will consult Lord Dinwiddie about your rebellious attitude, Teresa! I suspect he will agree with me completely and refuse to allow you to stay behind," Lady Cranfield said as she turned to leave the room.

"I consider Lord Dinwiddie a right-minded, most reasonable man, Lady Cranfield," huffed Sir William, as he struggled to his feet, bolstered by his newly discovered ardour, "but to further influence his decision you may tell him that I intend to marry Miss Bidwell!"

"William!" Her beloved's name fell from Teresa's lips in an almost reverent tone.

By now Kitty was beginning to enjoy the theatrics enormously. She didn't feel as if she were an intruder in this drama, for no one took the least notice of her. The other occupants of the room were so caught up in their various emotions that she might have been a gnat on the wall. By remaining completely silent, she hoped to remain invisible and thus be allowed to behold the conclusion of these stirring events.

Lady Cranfield's countenance had at first grown red upon hearing Sir William's declaration, but had steadily deepened till it was now a regal purple. She spluttered spasmodically, and Kitty began to be seriously concerned lest Lady Cranfield fall into a dangerous swoon. And who in the room would have the strength to catch her if she fell? Or to drag her to the couch if she were to collapse to the floor? Oh, where was the earl when he was needed?

But Kitty's fears were ill-founded. Lady Cranfield did not intend to make an uncomfortable resting place of the hard floor, or suffer the inconvenience of a swoon when she had a schedule to keep. Bottling her indignation and amazement with some success and removing all trace of emotion from her countenance and voice, she said, "I wash my hands of you, Teresa. Perhaps you have been the evil influence who turned my daughter against me, after all. I bid you good day, and good riddance!"

Kitty considered Lady Cranfield's words very unfair and was about to say so, but when she glanced over at Teresa she discovered that defending her friend would be unnecessary. Even before Lady Cranfield's heavy footsteps ceased to echo down the hall, Teresa had rushed to her favourite invalid and gently, wordlessly pushed him back onto his pillows. She then knelt on the floor in front of him and pressed his hand against her cheek. A look passed between them that was filled with such tenderness that Kitty could no longer justify her presence. The moment was theirs and should be viewed by no one else. Smiling happily and brushing a sentimental tear from her eye, Kitty exited the room as quietly and unheeded as a church mouse.

IF LADY DINWIDDIE was made unhappy over Agatha's abdication of the grand position as Countess of Hatherleigh, the realization that plain Miss Bidwell had stolen an advantageous marital catch right out from under the nose of her beautiful godchild made her positively wretched. She took to her bed and refused to see anyone, even neglecting to bid her sister goodbye when that lady huffed disdainfully into her carriage and instructed her coachman to "Drive with haste, Jed! I will be away from here with all due speed!"

She condescended to allow Lord Dinwiddie to kiss the air above her outstretched hand and pulled her mouth into a semblance of a smile, but that gentleman did not seem to mind. In fact, as Kitty watched Lady Cranfield's departure from an upper window, she detected a rather cheerful expression on Lord Dinwiddie's face as he stood in a cloud of dust to wave the carriage away. Then, as he looked up at her, grinning and nodding conspiratorially, all doubt was removed from her mind. She laughed down at him, then withdrew to her room to contemplate the future.

Two days passed with excruciating slowness. With the new lovers desiring no one's company but their own, and only the occasional intervention of Perkins forcing Miss Bidwell to get some rest, and Lady Dinwiddie's self-enforced seclusion, Kitty found she was left to her own devices. Lord Dinwiddie kept mostly to the library and Kitty was reluctant to intrude upon his solitude. When they met in the hall, or even at the dinner table, Lord Dinwiddie spoke sparingly and on the most innocuous subjects. But his general air was in curious contrast to his silence. He reminded Kitty irresistibly of a cat who had just swallowed a mouse. His thoughts were apparently highly entertaining, but he did not intend to share them.

On the third morning after the earl's removal to the Black Swan, Kitty grew disgusted with her ennui and sought to make herself useful. She visited the Kimballs, and was pleased to find Johnny much improved. She passed the greater part of the day there, only returning in time to dress for dinner. She was better satisfied with herself when she returned, but knew a few moments of acute distress when her expectations of seeing the earl were disappointed again. Hiller announced in his blandest tones—as if it were not the most important thing in the world to her!—that the earl had not returned to Ridley Hall as yet.

Three days! It had been three days, she fumed to herself as she flung off her riding habit and kicked it into a corner of the room. Plopping down onto her bed with complete abandon, Kitty lay with legs and arms outstretched and stared glumly at the ceiling.

"For shame, miss!" called Leah reproachfully as she came into the room. "Throwing your pretty things onto the floor! Haven't you a thought to spare for your poor abigail! I've broken my back pressing this habit many a time!" She bent down to pick up the mistreated item, shook it out and returned it to the wardrobe before continuing to scold her mistress. "And lying about in your underthings! Why, anybody'd think you was playing the idle rich!"

She had begun to be sorry for throwing her garment on the floor—she did not wish to make extra work for Leah—but when Leah began to berate her for lying on the bed, Kitty's mouth set into a line of stubbornness and she would not apologize. She rolled over onto her side and closed her eyes, drawing her knees up into the childish position she resorted to in times of distress.

Leah must have recognized the symptoms, because she clicked her tongue and threw a quilt over

Kitty's shoulders, saying, "I'll tell his lordship you're not feeling up to dinner tonight, miss. You get a wink of sleep and things'll look better." She patted Kitty's shoulder affectionately and left the room.

Even this small show of sympathy was enough to undo Kitty. She felt the warm trickle of a tear down her cheek, and then another, and another. She fell asleep with the earl's name on her lips and wondered why he did not come.

CHAPTER TEN

WHEN KITTY AWOKE her room was dark. She was covered in goose bumps and she wondered why Leah had not closed the window. But when she threw off the quilt and stood up to pull the latch to, she discovered the window was already securely shut. Then she realized that there was no chill in the air at all. The cold had no physical origins. Butterflies danced and swooped in the general region of her stomach, but, though she had missed dinner, she knew it was not hunger pangs that were causing the disturbance.

Her eyes were drawn inexorably to the window where she could see a golden three-quarter moon dancing on the horizon. Kitty sometimes wondered if she were a witch of sorts—hadn't the earl mentioned that she resembled one?—so strong was her sense of kinship with nature, the night, the wind, every part of mother earth's mystical, spell-binding beauty.

She unlatched the window and leaned out into the warm air for a few moments, then, no longer able to resist the lure of what might be one of the last summer evenings of the year, she lit a candle and dressed herself in the first gown that came to hand when she opened the wardrobe. It happened to be a white muslin that flared rather more at her ankles than most of her other gowns. It would be suitable for a walk to the lake. She glanced into the mirror above her dressing table and saw that her restless sleep had pulled her hair out of any semblance of order. Impatiently she pulled a brush through it several times, then left it loose, letting its glorious length fall naturally onto her shoulders and down her back.

As she left the room, she felt Cleopatra sliding past her through the door. She stopped for a moment to look down at her pet and lift an index finger to her lips, whispering in no uncertain terms that the cat must be as quite as a mouse. The clock struck ten as she slipped down the hall and left the house by way of a seldom-used side entrance. She took care to remove the key hanging on the wall so she might secure her later re-entry.

She was reminded of her visit to the lake a few weeks ago. She had found the earl there then, and her footsteps quickened on the paved walk until she found herself on the grass and almost running towards her destination. That other night the wind had been high, the sky cloudy with intermittent rain. Tonight the air was still and warm, crackling with expectancy.

The lake lay placidly before her and she approached the covered dock, thick with vines, with an eagerness for which she could only reproach herself, especially when she found it empty. At least she supposed it to be empty, since she heard nothing and could detect no movement at all in the darkness. Suddenly she heard a snort and a horse's hoof ring on the path. She whirled round and saw Lightning standing by a tree several yards away, his white-maned head bobbing up and down as if in greeting. Kitty smiled and turned first to the right and then to the left seeking the horse's master.

"I thought you would never come." It was his voice. Low and deliciously teasing. "Do you mean to stand there all night flirting with Lightning? I shall begin to suspect that you have designs on my horse similar to those I had on yours!"

Kitty discovered the earl sitting on a low rock at the edge of the lake. She walked forward a step or two and then she stopped. She was suddenly over-whelmed by shyness. Her heart beat so loudly that he must surely have heard it and wondered.

"Kitty, I will not eat you! Come here!"

"You are always ordering me about, my lord," she returned playfully, though her voice was soft and girlishly high. "Why do you not stand up and greet me like a gentleman?"

"If you must know, my girl, I am without shoes at the moment! I have no desire to puncture my foot on a rock in an effort to uphold England's code of po-lite behaviour," he returned dryly.

"You are without shoes?"

"Yes! Didn't I say so?"

"But why?"

"Because the water is wonderfully cool and I've been pacing up and down this end of the lake for the past two hours waiting for you!"

"I am to infer, then, that you are soaking your tired feet," she saucily rejoined, buoyed by his admission of having waited so long and so uncomfortably for her. She skipped the rest of the way over to him, sat down immediately on the grassy bank and proceeded to remove her own half boots as unselfconsciously as might be.

"You'll muddy your dress, miss," he observed in a half whisper.

"And pay dearly for it tomorrow when Leah finds out," she agreed, modestly pulling off her stockings with the hem of her skirt somehow secured around her ankles. She stretched her legs out and dabbled her feet in the water lapping gently against the shore. Cleopatra had followed and curled up against her back.

"I wish I might see your gown more clearly," the earl remarked with an odd intake of breath. "It looks to be white and you are so fetching in white!"

"I am sorry to disappoint you, my lord, but it is too dark!" Kitty lightly rejoined, though her throat constricted at the seductive tone which was so much more revealing than his actual words.

Lord Hatherleigh stretched behind him and pulled something out of a bag of sorts from behind the rock. Kitty heard a scratching sound and suddenly there was light. He'd lit a candle and now he held it in front of him and moved it up and down as if to see all of her.

Dazzled at first, she could see only the flame glowing against the darkness with its bright yellow aura and swirling, hypnotic tail. But when Lord Hatherleigh placed the candle on a rock next to him, the light softened and enveloped them in a pool of warmth. Her eyes adjusted and suddenly she could see him clearly.

The courage she'd borrowed from the darkness failed her now. Seeing his own dear face again, its masculine angles framed by those dark brows and thick, black hair, she felt more vulnerable than she'd ever dreamed possible. He'd discarded his jacket, and the open collar of his shirt exposed a strong column of neck and a small triangular patch of chest hair. Kitty shivered. In his disarray he was more desirable than ever.

But just seeing him would be endurable if only she could ignore the uncanny intensity of his eyes. He seemed to draw her very soul out with those eyes! She shifted her gaze downward to what she deemed would be a safer sight, downward to the lake and their feet dangling in the water. But she found no escape there. Below the buckskin breeches his calves were bare, the dark mat of hair on his legs intensifying that delightful, frightening chaos of her senses.

"You look like an angel in that gown, Kitty," he murmured. Then, seeming to shake himself, added laughingly, "But we both know that that is not the case!"

"If you are alluding to my conduct the night of the ball," Kitty blurted out, conscience-stricken and embarrassed, "you were quite as much to blame, you know! Kissing my fingers like that was really not necessary!"

The earl laughed. "Indeed not," he agreed, "but so diverting, don't you think?"

Kitty did not answer. She wasn't sure if she were angry with him or not. He was very entertaining, to be sure, but she had serious questions that needed to be answered.

"You are right, however," he continued, before she had made up her mind what to say or do next. "In fact, that evening's events were entirely my own fault, because even if you'd tried to slap me as you have tried before, I should have kissed you, anyway."

"Ah, but you did not kiss me," she corrected him, then blushed at the amused arch of his brow.

"Yes, Lord Dinwiddie's timing was . . . impeccable."

Kitty would not have described it thus. *Unfortunate* sprang to her mind, but she forbore to tell him her true opinion. "How did you know I needed to be rescued that night, anyway, my lord?" she asked him, determined to know it all, even if she must shame herself with direct interrogation.

"I saw you leave the ballroom followed by no less than four gentlemen, who later returned disappointed, and when I saw Whitchurch go out by the same way, I naturally became suspicious."

"And I am grateful to you for it," she told him earnestly and looked him directly in the eye.

"I would have killed him if he'd as much as touched you," the earl returned in an equally serious tone.

Shaken by the conviction of his words, Kitty grew uneasy and hurriedly changed the subject. "How did you know I would come here tonight? I thought you had gone, you know. You have been gone three days!" She felt her face flush at the accusatory note that had slipped into her tone.

He laughed, low and with pleasure. "I knew you would come because there is a strong bond of communion between us, isn't there, Kitty?"

She could not answer. She admitted to that bond but she hoped there would be more than that between them.

"It has been a weary three days for me, too, Kitty, but it could not be done otherwise, you know. It seemed indelicate to appear before your godmother, feeling as I did."

She turned her face away from him, snatching at a tuft of grass and throwing it into the lake. "You felt distraught, then?" she muttered.

"Felt distraught . . . ?"

"Well, about your fiancée, of course!"

"Oh, yes! That unfortunate business of running away with Cranfield! Now I understand you."

Kitty turned sharply to stare at him. "You are teasing me!"

"And why shouldn't I? You are asking ridiculous questions! How can you suppose I would feel anything but elation at knowing I was free?"

"Maybe I would not ask such ridiculous questions, my lord," she answered haughtily, so annoyed that she did not at once heed his last statement, "if you would not act so enigmatically! You have been gone three days! You have given absolutely no indication of your feelings for Agatha, or...or for me! What am I to think? What am I to do? Just wait patiently and, and... What did you say just now?"

"You are to think of no one and nothing but me, my love," he answered in a hoarse whisper, moving closer to her and pulling her fast against his chest. "And do nothing but this."

As the earl's lips claimed her own, all Kitty's doubts and frustrations over the past few days vanished in the exultant response that poured through her. His lips were soft, yet firm, and answered every question of her heart. She gave herself now, willingly, pressing against him with an abandon that must have taken the earl off guard, for suddenly he was pulling away from her and breathing in a queer, shallow way. Kitty stared at him, dazed and confused.

"I mean to be an honourable man, Kitty, and will not have the scandalmongers in the ton counting the days from our wedding to the birth of our first child. But if you continue to be so tempting..."

"But I am a flesh-and-blood woman, Nathan, after all," Kitty breathed, daintily biting his lower lip and sending a shiver through him. "And only a country chit, at that," she added mischievously. "I thought I was incapable of catching a city beau as experienced as yourself!"

"You caught me from the moment I saw you, love," he answered, kissing the tip of her nose, her brow and the soft angle of her cheekbone.

"Then why did you not come sooner, Nathan? I have been beside myself!"

"How could I be in the same house with you and not declare my love and my intention of marrying you, Kitty? And how would such actions seem when I had so recently been jilted by your godmother's niece?"

"And you imagined that three days would make a difference? I assure you, my godmother will be utterly delighted to know you want to marry me, especially since I have not succeeded with—" Kitty stopped short. It seemed indelicate to mention Sir William and her shameless pursuit of that gentleman while she lay happily in the earl's arms.

"What? And haven't you?" The earl laughed and squeezed his lady love with delight. "Miss Bidwell has won the day, I gather!"

"On the very day you left!" she admitted, astonished. "But how did you guess that, Nathan? I suppose you have had your man spying on us!"

"No, I have not. But I should have. One reason I have kept at a distance this long was to ensure that Sir William would have time enough to come up to scratch for the girl. I hoped that the old... I mean, Lady Cranfield, would leave within a day or two of my departure, and her decision would initiate a declaration from Sir William. But I must admit I thought it would take longer!"

"And have you had this entire thing planned from the beginning?" she asked him, pulling away just as he meant to deposit a kiss on her chin. "What about our wager?"

"Entered into for the sheer fun of it, my darling. I had no intention of ever allowing you to succeed and took great pains to see that you did not."

"But what if I had?" she insisted.

"Kitty, darling, you could no more be a patient, doting mother-wife to Sir William than you could fly to the moon, and that is precisely what he wanted! Miss Bidwell is perfect for him."

"But are you saying I could not be a good mother, Nathan? For if you are, I cannot imagine why you should wish to marry me!"

The earl leaned slightly forward, cradling Kitty in his arms, her head resting against his shoulder. "I've no doubt you'll be all that is most endearing as a mother to our children, Kitty." He kissed her and

Kitty began to wonder how soon they might begin that delightful process of becoming parents. "And," he continued, leaving her a moment to catch her breath, "anyone seeing you with the Kimballs and their little ones might see your wonderful capacity for compassion and warmth."

"So you think I have some redeeming qualities, after all," Kitty whispered, her brows knitting thoughtfully. "But I still must know more, Nathan."

"Anything, my love. But we had better stand up, because whilst we're in this position my mind has a tendency to wander."

They stood up, and the earl pulled her against him. She rested her head against his shoulder for another moment, breathing in the fresh soap and masculine scent of him, then said, "You know, I think Lord Dinwiddie has known how it would be all along."

"Yes. I believe that astute gentleman has perceived my dilemma from the very beginning," the earl agreed.

"You never did love Agatha, then?" Kitty looked into his face, needing to know.

He shook his head, smiling tenderly at her. "I did not deem it necessary to do so. She seemed well suited to fill the role of Countess of Hatherleigh. And since our parents had wished for the match, I thought I might marry Agatha as easily as any other well-born attractive female. Love was never a consideration."

"Then I need not feel guilty about Agatha, I suppose," Kitty observed, still frowning.

"And why should you? She is happy now. And I must thank you for your efforts in that area, as well, Kitty. I did not expect the elopement. I only hoped that she might cry off from the engagement once she discovered she was in love with her stepbrother. I kept hoping that Cranfield would make a push! Thankfully your, er, intervention hastened the deed!"

Kitty blushed. "You mean my meddling!"

"Do not blush, my dear. It is all to the good! Are you satisfied now?"

But another thought had occurred to Kitty and she said, "But what about my family, Nathan? Do you not abhor being connected to Benjamin in any way?"

"I shall take great delight in being related to him, Kitty, my love," the earl grimly acknowledged, "for I shall lend him money and threaten him with collection of it whenever he misbehaves. In this manner I shall hope to alleviate some of the distress which his despicable behaviour causes his poor wife!"

Kitty smiled and the earl, entranced by her expression, kissed her again. "Oh, how I repented of my foolishness in securing Agatha's hand in marriage, but how could I know I would meet you, Kitty? You are beautiful, but with a mind and heart to match. And wit! Your acerbic tongue will infuriate and delight me, my enchantress. Once we are married you will lead me a merry chase, I've no doubt! Have you any more questions for me? Is there anything more you need to know before declaring yourself willing and able to be my wife, Kitty, before these witnesses—the sky, the lake, and this black witch's companion at our feet?''

"Only one," she admitted timidly, lowering her head to stare unseeing at his shirt buttons. "Do you love me as I love you?"

"And have I been so dim-witted as to have omitted such a declaration, Kitty?" laughed the earl, throwing his head back and exulting in the moment. "I love you more, my dear, than you will probably ever know."

Satisfied at last, Kitty decided that the best way to signify her consent was to indulge with delight her beloved's desire to kiss her again and again. After a few moments of sheer ecstasy, the two were forced to acknowledge that strict chaperonage of lovers might indeed be necessary if the scandalmongers were truly to be foiled. They willed themselves to release each other and, laughing at the absurdity of it, pulled their stockings and shoes on over damp and sandy feet, then walked slowly but determinedly towards the house.

As they strolled arm in arm they eagerly talked of their plans. They agreed on a wedding date not more than a month in the future, each secretly wondering how they might stand not being completely together until then. When Kitty grew silent, the earl asked her what she was thinking of so intently.

"That orangutan in the menagerie in London," she admitted with an embarrassed smile. "I was thinking that I wished it might feel as free and happy as I do now."

"I shall ride post-haste to London," the earl declared with exaggerated passion, while Kitty giggled in appreciation, "buy the wretched creature for whatever exorbitant fee is required, and on our wedding day, Kitty, we shall release it to eat cake and play with the children. Then, when it has stuffed itself senseless, we will ship it away to Africa where it will be loosed again and allowed to roam amongst its fellows and be entirely itself!"

"As I shall be when we are married, Nathan?"

"I would wish you to be nothing but yourself, Kitty, entirely yourself. The only time I shall curtail your freedom, my dear, is when I shall lock you securely in my bedchamber each night. Do you object?"

Kitty did not object at all.

"WHERE IS KATHERINE? I finally resolve to leave my couch for some company to raise my spirits before I sleep, and she is not to be found! Leah says she does not know where Katherine is and seems insensible to her mistress's disappearance, for she had a foolish simper on her face when I asked her. And if her abigail declines to be alarmed, what am I to think? Arthur? Are you listening, my dear?''

''Oh, yes, dearest, I heard everything you said,'' his lordship assured her, twisting round in his chair and lowering the newspaper. ''But I don't think you should be concerned. Kitty is out by the lake.''

''Quite alone?''

''Oh, no. She is with the earl.'' Lord Dinwiddie resumed reading his paper as before.

''With the earl? What are they doing?''

''When I strode past them on a ramble a little while ago I observed him to be kissing her.''

''Kissing her?'' Lady Dinwiddie sat down immediately and put her hand to her chest, quite shaken.

''Yes. And he was doing it so thoroughly that they did not notice me in the least. In fact, I believe nothing could have disturbed them. Even Cleopatra, who was yowling jealously at their feet, did not seem to break their concentration. Prying them apart would have been beyond me, I assure you.'' He turned a page.

''Arthur, you must make the earl marry her!''

''Oh, I do not think *that* will be necessary!''

''Not necessary! She will be disgraced!''

''Oh, you misunderstand me, my dear. I agree they should marry, but I do not think I shall have to *make* them. I believe it has been the earl's intention to marry Kitty from the beginning.''

"From the beginning of what, Arthur?" Lady Dinwiddie was beyond astonishment now. She felt numb—surely nothing else could happen!

"From the moment he set eyes on her, I suspect."

"But I don't understand, Arthur," she wailed pathetically. "People are getting betrothed to the right and to the left of me and I did not see any of it coming!"

"Ah, do not underestimate yourself, my dear. Did not you say how well they complemented each other at the ball? Something about regal bearings or some such stuff? Perhaps you suspected how it would be even then."

"Why, I did say that, didn't I?" she agreed, somewhat mollified. She considered for a moment and began to see that it was all not so very incomprehensible as she had at first supposed. "Now that I think on it, Arthur, I've no doubt they will be very happy together!"

Lord Dinwiddie looked up over his newspaper, smiled affectionately at his wife and said, "Your judgement is unerring, my dear. That they will be happy is a certainty. And how could it be otherwise? They look so well together!"

"You are quite right, my dear. I don't know how I managed to overlook it for so long. Dearest Kitty," sighed Lady Dinwiddie, replete with happiness. "What an excellent godchild she is!"

Harlequin Regency Romance™

COMING NEXT MONTH

#33 SUSSEX SUMMER by Lucy Muir
When Captain Edward Tremaine returns from the
Peninsular War, the first sight to greet his weary eyes
is the natural beauty of Miss Jane Hampton tending
to her English country garden. As Jane and Edward's
friendship grows, Jane begins to nurture hopes for the
future. But Edward's sudden departure to London
and his subsequent return with the glamourous Lady
Julietta Blackwood do not bid well for her cherished
dreams.

#34 THE CALICO COUNTESS by Phyllis Taylor Pianka
Emily Merriweather Harding had little idea that when
she rescued the tipsy, grimy, aging ragamuffin from a
gang of youthful thugs, she had rescued a countess.
Claiming to have been lost at sea, the cantankerous
but loveable old gammer demanded to be taken home
to her beloved only son, James Carstairs, Earl of
Berrington. Needless to say, the earl was disbelieving
and when he demanded that Emily stay to "chaperon
her accomplice" she could hardly refuse!

**From America's favorite author
coming in September**

JANET
DAILEY

For Bitter Or Worse

Out of print since 1979!

Reaching Cord seemed impossible. Bitter, still confined to a wheelchair a year after the crash, he lashed out at everyone. Especially his wife.

"It would have been better if I hadn't been pulled from the plane wreck," he told her, and nothing Stacey did seemed to help.

Then Paula Hanson, a confident physiotherapist, arrived. She taunted Cord into helping himself, restoring his interest in living. Could she also make him and Stacey rediscover their early love?

Don't miss this collector's edition—last in a special three-book collection from Janet Dailey.

HARLEQUIN'S WISHBOOK
SWEEPSTAKES RULES & REGULATIONS
NO PURCHASE NECESSARY TO ENTER OR RECEIVE A PRIZE

1 To enter and join the Reader Service, affix the Four Free Books and Free Gifts sticker along with both of your other Sweepstakes stickers to the Sweepstakes Entry Form. If you do not wish to take advantage of our Reader Service, but wish to enter the Sweepstakes only, do not affix the Four Free Books and Free Gifts sticker to the Sweepstakes Entry Form. Incomplete and/or inaccurate entries are ineligible for that section or sections of prizes. Not responsible for mutilated or unreadable entries or inadvertent printing errors. Mechanically reproduced entries are null and void.

2 Whether you take advantage of this offer or not, your Sweepstakes numbers will be compared against a list of winning numbers generated at random by the computer. In the event that all prizes are not claimed by March 31, 1992, a random drawing will be held from all qualified entries received from March 30, 1990 to March 31, 1992, to award all unclaimed prizes. All cash prizes (Grand to Sixth) will be mailed to the winners and are payable by check in U.S. funds. Seventh prize to be shipped to winners via third-class mail. These prizes are in addition to any free, surprise or mystery gifts that might be offered. Versions of this sweepstakes with different prizes of approximate equal value may appear in other mailings or at retail outlets by Torstar Corp. and its affiliates.

3 The following prizes are awarded in this sweepstakes: ★ Grand Prize (1) $1,000,000; First Prize (1) $25,000; Second Prize (1) $10,000; Third Prize (5) $5,000; Fourth Prize (10) $1,000; Fifth Prize (100) $250; Sixth Prize (2500) $10; ★★ Seventh Prize (6000) $12.95 ARV.

   ★ This Sweepstakes contains a Grand Prize offering of $1,000,000 annuity. Winner will receive $33,333.33 a year for 30 years without interest totalling $1,000,000.

   ★★ Seventh Prize: A fully illustrated hardcover book published by Torstar Corp. Approximate value of the book is $12.95.

   Entrants may cancel the Reader Service at any time without cost or obligation to buy (see details in center insert card).

4 This promotion is being conducted under the supervision of Marden-Kane, Inc., an independent judging organization. By entering this Sweepstakes, each entrant accepts and agrees to be bound by these rules and the decisions of the judges, which shall be final and binding. Odds of winning in the random drawing are dependent upon the total number of entries received. Taxes, if any, are the sole responsibility of the winners. Prizes are nontransferable. All entries must be received by no later than 12:00 NOON, on March 31, 1992. The drawing for all unclaimed sweepstakes prizes will take place May 30, 1992, at 12:00 NOON, at the offices of Marden-Kane, Inc., Lake Success, New York.

5 This offer is open to residents of the U.S., the United Kingdom, France and Canada, 18 years or older except employees and their immediate family members of Torstar Corp., its affiliates, subsidiaries, Marden-Kane, Inc., and all other agencies and persons connected with conducting this Sweepstakes. All Federal, State and local laws apply. Void wherever prohibited or restricted by law. Any litigation respecting the conduct and awarding of a prize in this publicity contest may be submitted to the Régie des loteries et courses du Québec.

6 Winners will be notified by mail and may be required to execute an affidavit of eligibility and release which must be returned within 14 days after notification or an alternative winner will be selected. Canadian winners will be required to correctly answer an arithmetical skill-testing question administered by mail which must be returned within a limited time. Winners consent to the use of their names, photographs and/or likenesses for advertising and publicity in conjunction with this and similar promotions without additional compensation.

7 For a list of our major winners, send a stamped, self-addressed envelope to: WINNERS LIST c/o MARDEN-KANE, INC., P.O. BOX 701, SAYREVILLE, NJ 08871. Winners Lists will be fulfilled after the May 30, 1992 drawing date.

If Sweepstakes entry form is missing, please print your name and address on a 3" ×5" piece of plain paper and send to:

In the U.S.
Harlequin's WISHBOOK Sweepstakes
P.O. Box 1867
Buffalo, NY 14269-1867

In Canada
Harlequin's WISHBOOK Sweepstakes
P.O. Box 609
Fort Erie, Ontario
L2A 5X3

Offer limited to one per household.

© 1990 Harlequin Enterprises Limited   Printed in the U.S.A.   LTY-H890

COMING SOON...

For years Harlequin and Silhouette novels
have been taking readers places—but only in
their imaginations.

This fall look for PASSPORT TO ROMANCE,
a promotion that could take you around the
corner or around the world!

Watch for it in September!

★